DAVID A. ESTES

BLOOD
ON THE
WALL

Paperback-Press
an imprint of A & S Publishing
A & S Holmes, Inc.

ISBN-13: 978-1-945669-51-4

DEDICATION

For my daughters Ellen, Joni, and Jo Lyn–and their mother
Maxine who dances with angels.

Who is this who lies beside me, first hated then loved, and loved again?
Whence cometh he, and whither goeth that I may follow?

PROLOGUE

Judea in the time of King Herod

From the Mount of Olives the countryside east of Jerusalem swept down to the Dead Sea. It vaulted over deep gorges and ravines carved out of the earth by untold centuries of wind and torrential rains that ruptured the soft limestone of the desolate wasteland.

By day, foraging sheep clung to the stony slopes, nibbling at sparse grass in the shadow of laurel and oleander shrubs. By night, outlined against a cloudless sky, fingers of gray smoke rose from the campfires in the gaping ravines.

Since the beginning of time, dissidents who incurred the wrath of tyrant kings sought sanctuary in the rugged wilderness of Judea, where man survived by animal instinct.

Romulo de Vincius, a deserter from the Roman contingent in Jerusalem, stared into a fire of sticks and dried camel dung that lit the musty cave. Flickering flames cast eerie shadows against the wall.

Romulo was not alone. Joining him around the fire, three fellow escapees sat in silence, each with his own thoughts, pondering what the future might hold. They were deserters from the Roman legion and, if captured, would be executed without ceremony. Contemplating the crackling flames were a slender, sharp-faced Greek named Dionysus, and two Roman legionaries who risked their lives to separate themselves from the tyranny of King Herod.

The older of the two Romans was a squat centurion, a tough-jawed nineteen-year legion veteran named Varisias. The other, Milineus, a handsome, outgoing young man, had served in Judea for a few months only as a member of the palace guard.

Beyond the cave opening rain began to fall. Rivulets of water sifted through the cracks in the limestone walls, trickling down the dusty incline past the fire.

Thieves, highwaymen, revolutionaries, and runaway slaves for centuries had sought asylum in such caves. Counting among them were the four deserters circling the fire. They too sought refuge in the wilderness, freedom from the ruthless Herod. Rebels were they, fugitives and protesters.

Across Romulo's mind flashed the image of Major Marcus Cassio. Relishing the rage he envisioned on the face of the vengeful Roman, Romulo allowed himself a wry smile.

Cassio, discovering Romulo's escape, would be delighted to bring him to heel. One day the two would meet again, and history would bear witness who brought whom to heel.

Romulo's reflections were interrupted by the voice of young Milineus.

"Where will it all lead?" said he.

"Let him who knows speak," said the Greek.

"But we are free, Dionysus!"

"What is freedom?"

"He who never tasted wine," Varisias put in, "savors most the flavor."

"I don't want to think about it now," said the Greek.

"Nor do I," said Mlilneus. "For me it is a time for sleeping."

"Well said," Varisias agreed, using his helmet for a pillow.

Alone with his musings, Romulo searched for an answer to Milineus's quandary. Though he found none, he gave no thought to returning to his command. To do so would result in his being run through, likely by the hand of one who was once a friend. He added a stick to the fire, his body relaxed against the wall, and he slept.

Beyond the mouth of the cave, rain continued to fall.

Sometime in the night the refugees were jarred awake by blood-curdling screams shattering the stillness.

The four refugees grabbed their weapons and waded into the half dozen ruffians swarming the cave. Wielding crude tree-limb clubs, the intruders attacked with flailing blows. The fugitives countered with slashing strokes of their short swords. The encounter left the attackers swaddled in their own blood.

Young Milineus also did not survive the melee. His comrades buried him in a far corner of the cave, and marked the grave with a mound of stones.

The deserters stripped the assailants of their robes, and flung their bodies over the edge of the cliff. Ricocheting off the wall, the bodies landed with toneless thuds on the canyon floor.

"We have lost a comrade," said Romulo. "And we can be sure we have not seen the last of such encounters."

Dionysus agreed. "There will be others," he said with a solemn nod.

"More severe than this one most likely," Varisias said.

"If we are to protect ourselves and rescue Judea from the clutches of the tyrant, we will need help."

"Rescue Judea?" said Romulo, regarding the Roman with new respect. "I would have thought you'd be gone at the first opportunity, thinking only of saving yourself."

"If we don't save Judea," said the centurion with a shrug, "what good is our escape?"

"Would you wish for a Saul," said Romulo, "or maybe David?"

Varisias flashed a big-toothed grin. "I would gladly accept Gideon," he said. "Or a Joshua would be welcome."

"Joshua?" said Romulo. "You know Jewish history?"

"Not much, though I have long admired the courage of the Judeans."

Perhaps, Romulo mused, under the centurion's rough exterior dwelt a sensitive soul of more substance than he had thought.

"I must confess," Varisias went on, "that saving Judea was not my first notion."

"Then why are you still here?" said Romulo.

"Where would I go?" said Varisias, spreading his massive arms in a gesture of resignation.

"Rome is everywhere. I'm as well off here as in another place."

From a leather pouch Romulo brought a round of barley bread and tore it into three pieces.

One he gave to the Greek, another to the Roman, saving the third for himself.

"The emperor is far away," Varisias said, stuffing his mouth with a chunk of bread, "so I can abide him. But, like you, I detest the evil Herod. I have a son back home, and my greatest joy, aside from seeing him again, would be to carve the throat of the blood-thirsty king with a jagged blade."

Romulo poked a stick at the glimmering flame, seeking answers to what lay ahead for his companions and himself.

They had no arms, except for the short swords now hidden beneath the robes stripped from the slain assailants. They had no mounts, and no provisions aside from the pouches of bread and grain with which they had been able to escape. They were deserters, equipped only with a burning desire to rid Judea of the tyrannical Herod and his Roman masters. History recorded no victory, Romulo reflected, won by desire alone. Where on earth was there a fighting force capable of challenging the might of the Roman legions?

"The army will come," Varisias said, as though reading the thoughts of his friend.

"You, Captain Romulo," the Greek put in. "You are the one who must lead us."

"But, how many Romans can three deserters kill?"

"They will come," Varisias said.

Dionysus agreed. "If we feed the children their fathers will come."

Romulo turned to the corner of the cave where lay the body of the fallen Milineus. He studied the mound of stones, seeking answers to the young guardsman's question: Where will it lead? Returning to face his friends, Romulo said," Judea will remember you for this."

"No Roman," Varisias said," will now be safe in the land of Judea."

The Greek laughed at the irony of the centurion's threat.

Romulo laughed with him. Still, for him it was a solemn moment. There was no such thing as a short war. He didn't look forward to a long one.

PART ONE

CHAPTER 1

Bethlehem

Shira bas Haran trudged along the rocky path leading home to Bethlehem.

Absorbed in fear of danger to her infant son Jabal, her thoughts were disrupted by the voices of Roman guards barking orders at a column of men being herded to the prison compound.

"Romans!" she hissed. "Will they never be gone?"

Shira spent the day bending her slender body gleaning behind the reapers, collecting in her straw basket grains of barley fallen from the sheaves. Driven home by approaching darkness, she picked her way along the trail with field mates.

All around her were bleating, romping sheep whose master urged them home for the night. In the field she was tormented by a nagging sense that her infant son Jabal was about to be taken from her. Only the year before she experienced a similar anxiety for her husband Ezlon. The following day Ezlon was gored by an ox, and died before she could reach him.

Nightmares of that horrible day persisted. Only last night Ezlon appeared to her in a dream.

"Fear not, Shira," said he. "I am with God, and God is with you."

"What about Jabal?" she pleaded, but there was no answer. As suddenly as he came, Ezlon went away.

Hardly aware of the women who gleaned beside her, Shira was even less attentive now as they chattered gaily along the rocky path to the village and home.

Anxious to reach the home of her friend Hannah, with whom she left Jabal while she labored in the fields, Shira quickened her pace.

"Shira, look!" a friend shouted.

Shira turned to see a middle-aged man breaking from the column of prisoners, staggering toward the group of women. His bare feet, lacerated by sharp rocks on the trail, were red with blood. His clothing hung in tatters, his face a mass of contorted pain.

"After him!" a Roman on horseback shouted, and three legionaries ran down the stumbling prisoner.

"Help me!" the escapee moaned, collapsing at Shira's feet. "Please, help me. I stole only to feed my family."

Shira dropped to her knees and reached out to the writhing captive. A Roman soldier shoved her aside, and laid hold of the fallen man. Joined by a second Roman, together they jerked the prostrate fugitive to his feet, stripped him to the waist, and held him while a third man lashed him across his naked back with a bone-tipped thong.

Every blow brought spurts of blood. Murmurs of pain escaped the victim's quivering lips. Twelve times the scourge fell before his blood-smeared body collapsed.

"He's done for, sergeant," said the burly soldier who wielded the whip.

Sergeant Quintas, sitting a black Arabian, spread his crooked mouth into a gap-toothed grin.

"Get him out of there!" he ordered.

Two soldiers grabbed the feet of the unconscious escapee and dragged him away.

"You people go on about your business," Quintas yelled to the horrified witnesses. "This has nothing to do with you," Quintas scowled as he rode away.

"Romans!" Shira said with a vengeful glare. "Will we never be rid of them?" Continuing down the path, she paused at the village gate to pay one of the denigrating tolls demanded by King Herod as tribute to Roman Emperor Augustus Caesar.

"Deliverance," Shira fumed, "is as likely as rain before morning!"

***

Rain in Judea was ever longed for but seldom seen. Miraculously, however, in the eighteenth year of the reign of King Herod, rain drenched the land on the day Shira was born, heralded by her father Haran as a good omen.

Like most Jewish fathers, he hoped for a son, but the arrival of his bright-eyed daughter brought great joy to the heart of Haran ben Saul.

He scoffed at friends who boasted of their sons, defiling their male offspring as "hairy-legged asses."

"What can they do," Haran challenged, "that my Shira cannot do?"

Shira's affection for her father was boundless, but never did she know such joy as the day she married Ezlon, the only boy she ever cared a whit about.

Jewish tradition denied her the privilege, but "with due respect," she questioned her father's proposal that she marry Rabbi Nathaniel's son Aaron. Aaron, Shira protested, was an oafish pest who cared little for anyone, except for himself.

"Ezlon would not be good for you," her father countered. "His family has nothing."

"With Ezlon I would wish for nothing more," Shira cried. "Please, father, do not shackle me for the rest of my life to that ox Aaron. I could not be more unhappy than bearing his children."

Her mother Naomi placed a hand of caution on her husband's arm. "Perhaps you could speak to Ezlon's father," she said. "What can be the harm?"

"Old Amos!" Haran bristled. "What if he says yes?"

"There would still be time to consider," Naomi said.

"Ezlon is a good boy," Haran conceded, "but he has nothing to bring to the marriage. My daughter cannot live forever on her dowry."

"Is that more important than our daughter's happiness?"

In the end, with her mother's support, Shira convinced her father that Ezlon was the only boy with whom she could be happy. In the first year of their marriage, Shira and Ezlon were blessed with the arrival of their son Jabal.

At age nineteen she was left alone to provide for her infant son. Only with the help of rent from her late father's pottery shop, along with the grain she gleaned from the fields, did they survive. Was Jabal now to be taken from her?

Hannah, twice Shira's age, gaunt and gray-faced, stood aside as Shira brushed past her into the house. "Is he all right, Hannah?"

"Jabal? Why, yes. He's sleeping now."

"Nothing happened to him?"

Hannah placed a comforting arm across the trembling shoulders of her distraught young friend. Drawing her to the doorway to the adjoining room, Hannah said, "There, you see? He's asleep on the bed."

Shira reached for her son. Touching him, holding his innocent warmth, still, she could not shed the fear that some dreadful calamity was about to rob her of her beloved son.

***

In the northeast corner of Jerusalem's Temple Square stood King Herod's Antonia fortress, a massive structure of mortar and stone, its walls reached sixty feet high. From its four corners, watch towers vaulted twenty feet above the walls, manned by Roman legionaries charged with securing the safety of the paranoid king, who lived in constant fear of assassination.

For visiting dignitaries the Antonia provided elaborate accommodations: bathing pools, private quarters, and ornate halls for entertaining. Even now in the Great Hall, guests from throughout the empire gorged themselves on a sumptuous supper. Tables, set for thirty diners each, groaned under the weight of platters of roasted lamb served over hot coals, smothered with exotic sauces; roasted eels wrapped in beet leaves; oysters from the beds of the Mediterranean; bowls of steaming vegetables; baskets heaped with hot breads and fresh fruits; and imported wines that tantalized the palates of the king's honored guests.

An Egyptian prince wiped his mouth with a linen cloth, gesturing to his Syrian neighbor across the table. "One must admire the old rascal," said the Egyptian, ogling the sultry young women plying the diners with food and drink. "Herod is a master at putting on a feast."

"True," replied the Syrian. "It's too bad he's not here to enjoy it."

"Not here?"

"You didn't notice? Herod left long ago—without a word to anyone."

"Surely, he wouldn't just get up and go."

"But he did. I wouldn't be surprised if at any moment he stormed in here and ordered the lot of us to vacate the premises."

"Well, it's common knowledge the king hasn't been himself lately."

"Humph!" the Syrian scoffed. "Herod hasn't been himself since he murdered his wife twenty years ago."

"Oh, yes. Mariamne, wasn't it?"

"Mariamne," the other breathed with reverence. "The only one of his ten wives Herod ever cared about. And, as if killing her weren't bad enough, he also ordered his sons Alexander and Aristobulous put to death, charging them with conspiring with their mother against him."

"I remember," said the Egyptian. "I suspect he could have made the same charge against many of the people of Judea."

The Syrian nodded.

"You knew Mariamne?" the Egyptian said.

"I knew her–as loyal and charming a wife as could be. But, Herod fell victim to a vicious scheme of his sister Salome, who accused Mariamne of infidelity, and plotting to rob Herod of his power. Even so, he hasn't recovered from the death of Mariamne."

"Now, I hear the king has a new thorn in his side."

"Hmmnn," the Syrian grunted. "The babe born in Bethlehem."

"The one they call Jesus."

"The talk is that Herod fears him as a threat to his throne."

"Well, the king has overcome greater challenges."

"True. However, he is more vulnerable now," said the Syrian, "with his insatiable gluttony and excessive wine consumption.

"And, there's talk of some disease that's eating him alive. As if he didn't have enough to worry about, now he's obsessed with the notion that this Jesus will one day rise up and depose him as king of the Jews."

"But, he's only a small child. How could he be a threat to the king?"

"To Herod, everyone is a threat," said the Syrian. "Child or not, Herod ordered a search for the babe. If I know the king, he won't rest until this young Jesus is destroyed."

"Demented old coot!" the Egyptian snorted. "It's a wonder Caesar continues to support him."

"Demented he may be, but for over thirty years, Herod has been a staunch ally of the Roman Empire."

The Egyptian responded with a solemn nod.

The strains of lyre and lute, blended with the rhythmic beat of a wooden drum, filled the hall.

Among the tables slithered a dozen young women, swirling their transparent skirts, moving in seductive rhythm with the music. Their veiled faces and bare breasts stirred the loins of the glazed-eyed diners.

"Ah!" said the Syrian. "Herod does, indeed, know how to throw a party!"

***

Struggling to his feet, Herod reeled unsteadily from the hall, leaving his guests without so much as a by-your-leave, some of whom witnessed other such abrupt departures of the staggering king.

Discreetly cloaking sardonic smiles, the diners continued their revelry with hardly a pause in conversation.

Alone now on the Antonia's white-pillared portico, Herod paced its marble-tiled floor, his brow furrowed, his hands trembling.

Quaffing jellied wine from an ornate ewer at his side, he sought relief from the raging remorse tormenting his mind.

"Oh, my darling, my dearest Mariamne!" the king wailed into the darkness. "Great is the evil I have done you! Still, why do you not return, and restore the life blood that once flowed through these miserable veins?"

A loving wife, friend and confidante, Mariamne once shared the excitement of her husband's military and diplomatic triumphs. Herod became jealous and suspicious, trusting no one, ever fearful of being stripped of his power. In fits of rage, he executed thousands of Judeans, destroying anyone he suspected of threatening his throne. Even Mariamne once fled a threat of death by the incensed king.

"My beautiful, adorable Mariamne," Herod cried to her one long ago night. Cupping her face in both his hands, he pleaded, "What is it that troubles your innocent mind? Tell me, my dearest, what has torn you from me, that you no longer glorify my bed?"

"You need not ask," was her sharp reply, "since you already know the answer."

"What then? Can you not tell me what brings such sadness to your eyes? Never have I denied you any request. If there is anything I can do to relieve the sadness in your eyes, you need only ask."

"It is not what you can do, but what you cannot undo."

"Mariamne, Mariamne, you are my sanity, my love and my life. Without you I am nothing!"

She strode away, glaring at him with unabashed anger. "And now my sons and brothers, my father–even my grandfather Hyrcanus who wished for nothing, except to live out his life in peace–are nothing. All nothing!"

"Your grandfather? He was plotting against me. He left me no choice but to defend my position."

"You shed the blood of my family, and banished from my heart the love that I once felt for you!"

"My dear Mariamne!"

"I was proud to be your wife, to share your joy and your sorrow, to be the mother of your children; but you are now a tyrant, a blood-thirsty despot. You are not a king who governs with reason and compassion, but an animal who thinks only of his own survival. I can no longer pretend to be your wife!"

In a rush of passion Herod grabbed her, and crushed

her roughly to his chest. She did not protest. Once more, and once more only, would she endure his boorish embraces and his sweaty, flaccid body upon her, emptying himself for the last time of his vile desire.

Now, only the marble halls of the royal palace, once hallowed with love and affection, absorbed the mournful pleadings of the distraught king. From the grave he summoned those he most cherished, whose pleading voices resounded off the walls of his mangled mind. His anguished cries in the darkness of sleepless nights implored his dead Mariamne to rescue him from the hell he had created. To her, his beloved princess of the heroic Hasmoneans, his pitiful entreaties were endless. Even now, twenty years after condemning her to death, disease-ridden and dissipated, Herod ached, as forever he would, for the love and comfort of his precious Mariamne.

Haunted by the memory of his adored wife, terrified by the ghosts of the thousands whose blood he shed, Herod trod the path of the doomed, on guard at all times against death by poisoning or upheaval. At all hours of the night he roamed the deserted hallways armed with a sword, a pitiful captive of terror in his evil stronghold.

Herod sought justification for the slaughter of those Galilean revolutionaries, and their rebel leader Hezekiah. Justified, he assured himself, for that bloody encounter had brought him to the attention of Marcus Antonius, resulting in his appointment to the throne of Judea.

Rankled yet, however, that Hezekiah's son Judah had escaped the sword, and even now led guerrilla forces against the king's tyranny in the Galilee, Herod harbored hope that one day the point of his sword would pierce the heart of the elusive Galilean.

His gnarled mentality screamed that a king's obligation was to rule. Even those who despised his totalitarian methods, loathing his attempts to placate the Jews with outpourings of munificence–surely, he convinced himself, even they must sanction his responsibility to rule by whatever means necessary.

"Unworthy sons of jackals!" he now shouted into the night. With wine-blurred eyes, in the courtyard below he viewed an imaginary throng of adoring subjects, every gulp increasing the size of the crowd that only he could see. From his drooling lips flowed a stream of contemptuous epithets and self-serving entreaties, laced with threats to unworthy Judeans.

"In all my gracious majesty," Herod shouted, "have I not preserved your precious city? Have I not constructed aqueducts through which flow life-giving waters from the pool of Siloam? Have I not rebuilt your temple once desecrated by Crassus and Pompey? And from the depths of my compassionate heart, do I not allow you the freedom to practice your religious rites without restraint?" With a sheepish chuckle he admitted to himself, "Well, perhaps not totally, for there are times when even a king must exercise parental discipline."

Languishing in self-imposed solitude, with no thought of his guests, Herod indulged his gluttony with ambrosia and other Roman delicacies from a food-laden table at his elbow.

"And now this...this so-called newborn king of the Jews..." Herod contemplated wearily, news of whose birth plagued him to the point of distraction. At the top of his voice, he condemned all who would oppose him in favor of the babe born in Bethlehem. On the edge of hysteria Herod assaulted the air with clinched fists. "There is only one king of the Jews," he shouted, "and that is the one who now occupies the throne in the imperial palace! I, Herod the Great, am–" –cough, cough– "and forever shall be...king of the Jews!"

Feebly he bent his bloated body, acknowledging the wild cheers of his imaginary subjects whom, only moments before, he had berated without mercy. "Hail Herod!" he heard them shout, "our beloved king!"

Even so, Herod could not dismiss the threat of the baby Jesus, furious that he was not delivered as he had commanded. Had he not instructed those three kings who came in dead of night searching for the babe, to return with word of his whereabouts? And had he not assured them that he, too, wished to worship him who many believed to be the messiah? Yet, because they had foreseen, and foiled, his deceptive ploy, Herod secretly admired the perception of the kings who wisely suspected that his wish had not been to worship Jesus, but to destroy him. They, Herod conceded, had proved themselves no less cunning than he.

Through bleary eyes he peered into the dark streets beyond the fortress where lay the soundless city, silenced by debilitating curfews and decrees against assembly that fueled the flames of Judean defiance.

The Judeans' refusal to accept him, an Idumean, as a Jew tormented the warped mind of the vassal king. They despised his groveling allegiance to Rome, deploring his contempt for the authority of their Sanhedrin. Still, he continued to exacerbate their revulsion by defying Jewish law when dealing with rivals and lawbreakers, condemning them to the dungeon, selling them into slavery, even burning them alive.

Once a leader of commanding presence, skilled diplomat, and shrewd military strategist, Herod had been the unchallenged potentate of Judea. Staffed by admiring servants, and aides eager to do the bidding of the stalwart king, the Antonia had been the center of power and authority. Now, trusting no one, given to maniacal tirades, Herod dismissed aides whose loyalty he questioned. And the domestic staff now served out of fear of retribution, rather than with the pride and admiration with which they once had regarded the king.

Betrayed by those he trusted, spurned by those he loved, and detested by those he ruled Herod lived in fear of death by the hand of some vengeful Judean who would have sacrificed himself for the pleasure of separating with a dagger the ribs of the spurious king.

Rebuilding the temple to assuage the irascible Jews served only to enhance their disgust for the pawn of Rome. Still, they swarmed to the temple to worship their God. Even now the king's nostrils were attacked by the acrid stench of the burning flesh of oxen, goats, sheep, and cattle sacrificed on the altar, whose blood flowed through trenches to fertilize the gardens of the temple priests.

"Damn you, Judea!" the king roared to the invisible throng, "you who are not worthy of my spittle!"

To his ears came the clatter of horses' hooves on the stone-paved courtyard below. "Aha! Major Cassio approaches," the king shouted with a triumphant cackle. "Now we shall see who is the true and only king of the Jews! No longer will you taunt me with this Jesus annoyance." He pounded his chest, coughed convulsively, gasping for breath. "I, Herod the Great, am, and forever shall be, king of the Jews! Remember that, Judea! Remember that!"

CHAPTER 2

Bethlehem

"God did not choose us to be laden like asses!"

Stirring a pot of lentil soup, Shira recalled again those defiant words of her dead father. Her mother Naomi had showered her with love and attention, but, it was from her father that Shira learned of politics, religion, tolerance and intolerance, resentment toward the hypocritical temple priests, and hatred of "Herod the Horrible."

In her father's pottery shop, Shira spent many hours of her childhood, fascinated by Haran's slender fingers caressing the clay, applying the spatula, transforming the shapeless glob into an attractive bowl or urn. Around the table at mealtime she listened, awed by her father's unabashedly renouncing the burden of tribute demanded by Herod and the temple priests, damning the interminable "spying, taxes, and humiliating curfews" heaped on the backs of Judeans by the pagans from Rome.

Sopping a chunk of Naomi's fresh barley bread in mutton gravy, Haran had bellowed, "If we do not assert ourselves, who then will bury our bones?"

Emphasizing his anger with defiant shakes of his artisan's fists, Haran had acknowledged Naomi's tolerant nods, and the wonder in the eyes of his beloved daughter, as approval of his rebellious harangues.

Recalling her father's inflammatory discourses, Shira despaired of how much longer Judea would be made to suffer domination by the detested Romans. Already it had been over sixty years since Pompey ravaged Judea with his Roman legions, desecrating the temple, laying waste the land. Subjected to fierce Roman control, the Jews had responded with the same contempt with which they now regarded the denigrating Herod.

Oh, yes, Shira reminded herself, there had been protests and uprisings of discontent, but Herod had crushed them all with the help of his Roman guard. Shira's father, fearless in his opposition to the king's bloody assaults, had been arrested for his fiery oratory, dragged away, and condemned without trial to the dungeon. Beaten, tortured, denied food and water for days, until Haran's hatred for the Romans could no longer sustain him. Breathing his last in the middle of a winter's night, he was buried in an unmarked grave. Naomi, only two months later, grieved herself to death.

Saddened by the painful recollection, Shira gave the soup a vicious stir and brushed a tear from her cheek. Was her severest pain yet to come?

***

In the cavernous corridor of the Antonia the click of iron-clad boots echoed off the marble tile floor, prompting a hawk-faced servant to appear on the portico, bowing low before the bleary-eyed Herod.

"Yes?" bellowed the king. "What is it?"

"A thousand pardons, your grace," the young man stammered, "but the major has arrived, and seeks an audience with his royal highness."

"Well, show him in, idiot! Show him in!"

"As you wish, sire," the messenger muttered, bowing his way out.

Into the presence of the king a moment later strutted the forty-year-old Roman,

Major Marcus Cassio. His black hair was cropped short in the Roman tradition, his eyes sought the florid countenance of the listing king. Cassio's steel-spiked helmet was tucked under his left arm, and in his right hand he held a leather riding crop that he slapped uneasily against his knee.

"Ah, my king!" Cassio cooed with an expression which, except in the presence of the king, would have been described as a smirk.

Before he was assigned to duty in Jerusalem, Cassio had served in a minor position on the staff of Augustus Caesar in Rome. Cherishing yet his association with the emperor, he regarded with haughty disdain the tyrant king. Perceiving himself to be on a level above Herod, to the major the king was more to be tolerated than idolized.

Herod suspected that Cassio's assignment was to observe his activities, reporting them to Rome. In deference to Augustus, however, daring not arouse the wrath of the ruler of the world, the king had not removed the haughty Roman major. His regard for Cassio was no more flattering than Cassio's for him. Even so, Herod had charged the major with the responsibility of locating and delivering to him the babe called Jesus.

Pinning the Roman with a glassy-eyed stare, Herod drew his bushy eyebrows together at a point above his sharp Idumean nose. "What can you tell me," said he with unsettling calm, "that I don't know already?"

Cassio anticipated with no joy the response of the tempestuous Herod upon learning of his failure to locate the child Jesus. Bracing himself against the inevitable storm, the major bounced the riding crop against his knee.

***

An hour earlier, the marketplace beyond the walls of the Antonia had been alive with traders, pilgrims who traveled many miles to worship at the temple, and caravaners transporting precious jewels, wines, and cloth from distant lands. Now, the bazaars stood in shuttered silence. No longer were heard the shouts of vendors berating haggling customers, and the heated challenges of prospective buyers' accusing the merchants of charging too much for inferior merchandise. Heard only was the occasional squawk of a restless camel, or a donkey's ignominious honk.

From the amphitheater beyond the marketplace rose waves of applause. A magnificent three-tiered structure, the theater stood as another of Herod's fruitless attempts to mollify the Jews, only a few of whom had seen the inside.

The king no longer attended the performances. During his last appearance months ago, the wine-soaked Herod had chosen the middle of the third act to empty his royal stomach from his private box, splattering shocked patrons below with an outpouring of smelly green bile, creating havoc among the theater elite. The committee of directors, facing the prospect of losing their heads in protest of the king's uncouth antics, concluded that death by the king would be less humiliating than social ostracism. Granted an audience, therefore, the committee humbly requested that the king exercise discretion in his choice of time and place for yielding to the need to regurgitate.

With their heads still attached, the directors had departed the king's chambers relieved by his favorable, breath-restoring response.

Never since had the royal box been occupied. Herod, however, felt no loss for his capitulation. His enthusiasm for the theater had been fueled only by his hunger for power, deeming his appearance among the theater elite politically expedient. He had preferred the solace of his favorite jellied wine, the milieu of his existence, to attending the theater's performances.

Since the royal box remained unoccupied, of course, his guests around the tables in the Great Hall dared not commit the social breach of attending without the king.

Though Herod's seat of honor in the dining hall was not now warmed by the flab of the royal posterior, no one suffered restraint for dining without him. The food and wine continued to flow, and the absence of the king was mitigated by the stimulating entertainment he left behind.

Peering into the night from the portico, Herod's wine-blurred eyes could hardly see the dimming torches on the theater stage. Nor was he aware of the waning applause signaling the end of the play

***

Captain Romulo de Vincius joined the rush to the theater exits. Elbowing his way clear of the crowd, he was hardly aware of a lean, brown-robed man with a pointed black beard who fell in step beside him. "Ah, captain!" the man said. "Romulo de Vincius, is it not?"

"I'm Romulo."

"The search, captain. What progress is being made?"

"The search?"

"For the babe. The one born in Bethlehem. The people sense that the king grows impatient."

"That is not my charge," was Romulo's terse reply

In his third year of service in Judea, Romulo was well aware of the Jews' hostility toward

Herod. Though his personal regard for the king was by no means lofty, still, Romulo was a member of the Roman legion, serving under Herod's command, and dared not involve himself in Judean politics.

"The greater concern, captain," said the man, striving to match Romulo's long strides, "is that if the babe is not delivered as Herod commanded, Judea may suffer even greater restrictions imposed by the mad king."

Romulo came to an abrupt halt on the torch-lit path. With a sharp look he challenged the inquisitive intruder, questioning why he dared approach a Roman officer with such audacity.

"If that should occur, captain," the man went on, "it is likely that Rome also would suffer."

"Are your words," said Romulo, "intended as a threat to the Roman empire?"

Melting quickly into the night, the other made no reply.

Pondering the stranger's somber warning, with a wry smile Romulo found himself enjoying the suspected discomfort of the wily Cassio, whose task it was to seek and destroy the babe, quaking now in the presence of the irate king. For the ingratiating Roman major, he could muster no compassion.

***

King Herod, his demonic mind in quest of self preservation, rejected all reason. The threat of being deposed, he counseled himself, justified any means necessary to thwart banishment, even by the infant whose whereabouts he had been unable to discover. Sacrifice of human life was no deterrent to the fiendish despot's need to insulate himself against the loss of power. Slaying a mere babe, therefore, would be as nothing if it accomplished his obsession with preserving his sovereignty.

Herod's instructions to find and destroy the infant had produced nothing that eased his tormented mind, and Major Cassio's report of failure served only to compound the king's consternation.

"I do not want to hear of your failure," the king raged. "I want only to hear of your success!"

"But, sire, surely the great Herod knows–"

"Surely the great Herod knows," the king mocked, "that the major has a melon for a head. And surely the great Herod knows–"

My dear sire–"

"Silence, you bungling idiot!"

Reeling with fury, Herod was near to collapsing. Cassio moved to assist him, but the red-faced king shoved him aside, grabbing at a table for support.

"I charged you with the responsibility of finding and eliminating one tiny infant!" Herod seethed. "One small male child known to half the people of Judea. I put at your disposal a hundred, a thousand, as many of the palace guard as you required–even the emperor's legions if need be–to ferret out the person of one single infant. And after all this time, you have established no notion as to the whereabouts of the impostor to whom they refer as the new king of the Jews!"

"Of all the places we have searched, sire," Cassio said, "no child has been determined to be the one we sought."

"And where, major, have you sought?"

"Everywhere, sire. Bethlehem, Bethany, and beyond."

"And you have discovered the whereabouts of no such newborn king of the Jews?"

"None, sire."

"Then kill them all!"

"Sire!"

"Every male child under the age of two years you will destroy, major, or I will have your head!"

***

Pacing the courtyard of the Antonia, Major Cassio listened impatiently to an aide's recital of Herod's decree to the assembled troops..."As of this day and date," the aide droned from a parchment scroll, "Herod, king of Judea, does hereby order that all male children two years of age and younger shall be put to death with utmost expediency." The soldier re-rolled the scroll and tucked it under an arm, stepping back into ranks with a sharp salute which the smirking major did not acknowledge.

"You have heard the order of the king," Cassio screeched in his thin, high-pitched voice. "The search will begin immediately, and it will end only after every male child under the age of two years has been destroyed. You have your orders. Sergeant Quintas, dismiss!"

The troops dispersed, and Cassio came face-to-face with Romulo de Vincius. Romulo had stood apart, anticipating a confrontation with the major.

"Need I remind you, captain," Cassio said, "that you will be especially diligent in your search of Bethlehem?"

Repulsed by the major's arrogance, and by the gruesome task to which he was assigned, Romulo found no reason to alter his disregard for the Roman major.

"May I speak frankly, major?" Romulo said.

"You may, if you keep it short."

"I don't consider this assignment worthy of a Roman officer. The regulations state that—"

"Do not quote to me the regulations, captain," Cassio shot back. "I am well aware of their content and their intent." He emphasized his words with slaps of the riding crop against his knee. "I trust that your objection is not meant to convey a refusal to obey a direct order, captain, for if it is—"

"Major, I—"

"—I could have you flogged for insubordination. I could

break you to the rank of private." The corners of Cassio's mouth twitched, and his eyes flashed with anger. "I could have you stripped and shackled in the public square," he screamed, his shrill voice rising with each new threat. "I could crucify you, or bury you alive!" He paused, his face aflame with exasperation."Do I make myself clear, captain?"

Romulo's steady gaze bore into the eyes of the enraged Roman. "As you say, major," he said, "I have my orders." Slapping his knee with the riding crop, Cassio strutted away. Romulo's resentment mounted with every step that lengthened the distance between himself and the squeaking major.

***

Along the narrow winding cobblestone street the sandaled feet of young Simon ben Guron carried him in frenzied haste. Learning of Herod's decree, Simon's mother had sent him to alert her friend Shira. Through the marketplace he flew, spinning past heavy-laden donkeys, colliding with hawkers of wares, shoving his way through the mass of haggling buyers and shouting vendors. Upending a cartload of pomegranates, Simon waved off its owner's stream of epithets that followed him around the corner and along the street toward the modest home of Shira bas Haran. Still some distance away, Simon called, "Shira! Shira!"

Shira sensed that the usually unflappable Simon sounded in a fury. She dashed to her door, threw it open and saw the boy skid to a stop."What is it, Simon?" she said.

"The Romans, Shira. They're coming!"

"How can they come when they are already here?" Noting the fear in the eyes of the boy, she said, "Simon, why are they coming?"

"To kill the babies!" he shouted, dashing away.

With a bewildered shake of her head, Shira turned back into the house."To kill the babies?" To kill the babies! "Jabal!" She rushed to the bed where her baby lay asleep, swept him into her arms, and raced toward the stairway leading to the roof.

She heard a loud knock at her door. She hesitated. Should she answer it? Or should she—

She saw the door pushed open and in stood a Roman soldier. He looked at Shira as if surprised that she was there with an infant in her arms.

"You are—" the man said, checking a parchment list, "Shira bas Haran?"

Behind him, outside the door, bearing a metal-tipped lance, stood a second legionary, holding a scroll. Beyond the open doorway Shira could see a third Roman on horseback, peering in through the door, as though observing what was taking place.

"I'm Shira," she said. "What is it you want?" Jews viewed the Romans with deep-rooted suspicion and loathing. They worshiped their God, and hated the pagan occupiers.

"It has come to the attention of the authorities," the Roman said, "that you have a young son."

She clutched Jabal closer. *Only nineteen years old, would I have an old son?*

"I have a son, yes," she said. *Fool! Can't you see the baby in my arms?*

"And he is not yet two years of age?"

"Jabal?" How would this Roman know how old her baby was? "You mean my baby Jabal?"

"If that is the name by which you call him, yes. Jabal."

"What about my Jabal?"

She was beside herself with fright. Was this something about the fear that had plagued her senses—the fear that some tragedy was about to happen to her son? Young

Simon's warning—What was this about Jabal?

"Have you not heard?" he said.

"Heard?" she said. "Heard what?" On the edge of panic, she waited for the soldier to explain.

"The king's decree," he said.

From the street burst the horrified screams of women, and the wails of small children, punctuated by the rumble of hobnailed Roman boots pounding the cobblestones. Shira took a step toward the door to learn the cause of the commotion, but was barred by the Roman's outstretched arm.

"What decree?" she cried.

"Antillus," he said.

The soldier bearing the scroll stepped forward. He unrolled the scroll and, in a toneless voice recited, "As of this day and date, Herod, king of Judea, does hereby order that all male children two years of age and younger shall be put to death with utmost expediency." Antillus re-rolled the scroll and resumed his position.

"Put to death? Why?" she cried.

"It is not my lot to explain the purposes of the king."

Shira's trembling hands went to her face. "Surely there is some mistake. My baby Jabal is to be put to death? Why? What has he done?" Between wracking sobs, she cried, "He wants you to murder my innocent baby—and it is not your lot—to explain the purposes of the king?"

"Sergeant." The authoritative voice came from the doorway.

Shira saw there the man she had seen on the horse outside her door. He was wearing the uniform of a Roman officer. Black leather boots nudged his knees. At his side was sheathed a dagger with a curved blade, the favorite weapon of the Romans.

The sergeant snapped to attention in the presence of the officer.

"Step outside," the officer said.

"Yes, sir," said the sergeant, doing as he was told.

"You are Shira bas Haran?" the officer said calmly.

"Yes," Shira said.

"Did the sergeant tell you why we are here?"

"He said my son is to die, but he didn't tell me why."

"It is the order of the king."

"It is the order of the king!" she spat. "Has your king no decency? Is he so heartless that he must murder innocent children who don't even know there is a king?"

The officer glanced about Spies were everywhere. A critical word falling on the wrong ears could condemn him to the cross.

"You may have heard of the babe called Jesus born here in Bethlehem," he said, hardly above a whisper.

"The babe. Yes, I know about that."

"It has been reported that some believe he is the Deliverer, come to free the Jews from bondage." He took another wary look around. "Others proclaim him the new king of the Jews."

"What has that o do with my baby?"

"It is feared by the king that if enough people accept this Jesus as the newborn king of the Jews–"

"So," Shira said in agonized disbelief, "my baby is to die because of a sick, demented old man who is afraid of losing his kingdom to a babe!"

"Herod ordered that a search be made for the child, but he has not been found. Now, he has issued a decree that all male children under two years of age be destroyed."

"He's afraid my baby Jabal might be the new king of the Jews?"

"We have our orders," he said, motioning his comrades to take the child. "We must proceed."

"Wait!" Shira pressed a hand to his chest. "Please!" she cried. "He is so small, so soft and innocent. Have you no sons? Have you known the pain of having a son taken from you?"

"There are others," he said, gently removing her hands, "and time is short."

"My husband was gored by an ox and no longer lives. Please, sir, my son Jabal–he is my only joy. Surely, your own mother–"

"Silence, woman!"

"What of her love for you?"

With a sharp gesture the Roman officer instructed his comrades to take the infant.

Horrified, Shira struggled to hold onto her son. She tried to pull away but the man called Antillus tore her wailing child from her bosom and whisked him away.

"Jabal!" she cried.

Again she ran to the door, and again was restrained, this time by the officer standing in her way. For a brief moment their eyes met. He then withdrew his arm and joined the others.

"Murderers!" Shira screamed after them. "Godless Roman murderers!"

Exhausted, she crumpled to the floor, buried her face in her hands, and wept. In her ears echoed the words of her father: "If we do not assert ourselves, who then will bury our bones?"

CHAPTER 3

To be a Jew and not be free was unthinkable.

For sixty years Judea resisted the domination of the pagans from Italy to which other nations passively acquiesced. The Judeans' nationalistic spirit, explosive nature, and devotion to their God bolstered their resistance to Roman control. Only they, of all conquered peoples, opposed them, and the Romans didn't understand why.

To accomplish Caesar's desire for peace in Judea, Herod constructed glittering cities and rebuilt the temple, striving in vain to placate the irascible Jews, succeeding only in compounding their resentment of the vassal king. Over the years Herod had won the favor of the world's most powerful men–Julius Caesar, Marcus Antonius, Crassius, and now Augustus Caesar–but found no means by which to mitigate the indignation of the unforgiving Jews.

Herod's brutal extinction of any threat to his authority poured salt into gaping wounds, deepening the chasm between himself and those he ruled. And the blood that dripped from the blade that felled their beloved Mariamne could never be cleansed from the hands of the despicable king.

Now, fearing the prophecy that in tiny Bethlehem would be born one who might banish him from the throne, Herod had further poisoned the soup served his subjects by ordering the slaughter of innocent male children, invoking the pain of death upon the modest household of Shira bas Haran.

***

Shira did not know at what point in her grieving, her exhausted body succumbed to the need for rest. When she awoke, her vision was clouded by the darkness filling the room. Knuckling sleep from her eyes, she was stunned by the flicker of a candle in the hands of someone whose face she could not see. Puzzled, she rose to her knees as the light drew closer, outlining in its yellow glow a face she had seen before. Where? When?

Then, as lightning rends the desert midnight, her mind raced back to the afternoon. Jabal! Her baby Jabal! That man—the one on whose face the candle now cast an eerie glow—the officer! The Roman officer who stole her baby away!

By animal instinct she pulled herself to her feet and hurtled headlong toward the yellow flame. Flailing away with uncontrolled anger, she berated the detested Roman with a rash of flying fists and shouted insults.

He dropped the candle to the floor, grabbed her wrists, and forced her hands to her sides. With soft spoken words he tried to soothe her anger. She heard none of them until he said, "Please, allow me to release you."

"Do not release me," she hissed, "unless you are prepared to die as my son died by your evil hand!"

"Your son did not die by my hand," he said.

For a fleeting moment Shira felt hope that Jabal had been spared. But then she heard the Roman say, "It was by an order of the king that your son died."

"Hah! The fox blames the jackal for deeds of its own!"

"I cannot plead innocence in the death of your son," he said. "That's why I have come back." He relaxed his grip on her wrists, and she burst angrily away. "Please," he said, "it was not my wish to bring sorrow to your home."

She glared at him with hate-filled eyes, cheeks red with rage.

"My name is Romulo de Vincius," she heard him say.

Like the echo of a fading dream his voice came to her—like the hollowness of some ethereal thing that she could neither see nor touch. Yet, in her bereaved consciousness she knew it was not a dream. Her son was slain because he was not yet two years old to satisfy the fanatical whim of an insane beast. And here, standing before her with pleading eyes was the man who carried out the sentence—the body from which came the voice that sounded far away.

"I'm a captain in the Roman legion," Romulo said. Retrieving the candle from the floor, he placed it on the pedestal. "In the legion we are trained to be proud, to be tough, and to believe that we are invincible." He paused, sorting out the thoughts tumbling through his mind, searching for words he hoped would help her understand. "But now I am neither proud nor invincible. Most of all, I am repulsed by the task I was assigned to carry out here today."

Listening in stony silence, Shira's eyes bored into his.

"Throughout the land," Romulo said, "there is much sadness because of Herod's decree, and my comrades talk of revolt. Some were so distraught that they fell on their swords, and took their own lives."

"God go with them," she said mechanically. Then, driven by a surge of vengeance, she spat, "And have you similar plans for yourself?"

"I hope to avoid that," he said, "by seeking your forgiveness."

"Forgive you?" She was aghast. "Forgive you! The proud Roman seeks forgiveness of the lowly Jew!" With wracking sobs, she said, "You murdered my son, and now you expect me to forgive you? How could you have the gall to even suggest such a thing?"

"Because I can't live with the sadness that fills my heart."

"What about my sadness?" she cried, choking on the words.

"Earlier you mentioned my mother. Both she and my father were taken from me because they refused to worship Caesar as a god. They were thrown into prison. They died there, Shira."

She was startled that he called her by name. Even so, her eyes flashed with contempt for the repentant Roman."There were others, you said, and time was short. Have they forgiven you? Why have you come to me?"

"In the marketplace I have seen you with your son, holding him, loving him. I've wondered if my mother loved me as much as you loved him."

She strode away from him, her face flushed with anger."You Romans take lives," she stormed, "and now you ask me to spare yours!"

"Is that your answer?"

She flung the door open. "Leave my home!" she said.

Romulo straightened to rigid military attention. "As you wish, madam," he said. At the doorway he paused, his eyes meeting hers."When I was a young boy in Rome," he said, "I was fascinated by the parades on the Palatine. The sleek black stallions in their glistening gold and silver, prancing to the beat of the drums. The legionaries were decked out in colorful tunics, plumed helmets, and boots— shiny black boots that had never seen mud. Thousands of people lined the streets, and when the emperor rode past with his glittering entourage, all heads bowed in silence." In my bed at night I often lay awake dreaming of one day joining the legion, and being the proudest man in the empire. When I told my mother of my dream, she said, 'My son, if God had meant you to be a Roman soldier, he would not have endowed you with Jewish parents.'"

Shira cast him an astonished look. With a brief nod he left her pondering his bewildering revelation: A son of Judea with a Roman name?

***

Shira had thought there could be no greater sorrow than she had suffered at the death of her parents. Then, when Ezlon was taken from her, she learned how wrong she had been. And now, denied the joy of watching her son grow to manhood, her wretchedness knew no bounds. For weeks she raged, condemning the forces of evil that robbed her of her final happiness.

Try as she might, her friend Hannah could not relieve Shira's anguish. Put aside by her husband because she bore him no sons, Hannah could not share Shira's pain of having lost hers. But she tried, setting before Shira bowls of hot soup, plates of roasted lamb, and fresh baked wheat bread. She brought dates, sliced peaches, nuts, and sweet cakes that she knew Shira loved.

Shira pushed them all aside."Give them to the priests," she said. "Maybe then they'll have the strength to resist the Roman murderers."

"You must not speak so, Shira," Hannah chided.

"What can they do to me, Hannah, that's worse than what they have done already–crucify me?"

Even Rabbi Josef, whom Shira adored, and to whom she had turned in her earlier grief, was unable to comfort her. Tall and lean, with a yellowing beard that reached his waist, the aged teacher sat in her front room and watched her grind at the mill.

"I have not seen you at synagogue lately," said he.

"What has the synagogue to offer me?"

"The synagogue is the dwelling place of the Lord, my child, and where lives the Lord, lives the forgiving spirit."

"And what have I done that I should seek forgiveness?"

"The scriptures admonish that we are all sinners, and bid us attend worship to beg forgiveness for our sins."

"Hah! I pay my tribute. I gave you my son who, because of a jealous lunatic, no longer lives. And what have I received in return?"

"My heart is heavy for your loss, dear Shira, and those responsible for it shall receive their judgment. But, when we give to the Lord, we must remember that we have received our reward already. Our meager offerings are only in return for what he has given us."

"Is this it, teacher?" With a sweep of her hand she indicated the sparse furnishings of her modest home. "Is this the reward for which my son was torn from my bosom and bashed head first against the village wall? Is this all there is?"

"God works in mysterious ways, dear daughter. We dare not judge."

"Don't speak to me of rewards, Rabbi Josef. I am my own reward."

"In the arms of the Lord we find refuge from our grief."

"From my grief there is no refuge."

"As you wish, my dear," said the old rabbi sadly, taking his leave.

"As you wish!" Shira scoffed when he was gone. "As you wish!" she snorted again. Across her mind those supercilious words had echoed since first she heard them uttered by the condescending voice of that arrogant Roman,

Captain Romulo de Vincius. "As you wish, madam!" she fumed. Still, she could not deny that at times she wondered what had become of the Jewish boy who grew up to be a Roman soldier.

The answer came when the chill of autumn sent her scurrying to the marketplace for warmer clothing. Through mobs of frenzied shoppers she spun her way to the wool merchant's, her ears accosted by the shouted entreaties of the hawkers of wares and the haggling protests of prospective buyers. Rummaging through piles of fabric, she rejected most of what she saw. Finally, settling on a woolen cloak, she took it up, and paid the clerk who complained that he hadn't charged her enough. Turning to leave, she came face-to-face with Romulo de Vincius.

"Shira!" he said with a delighted smile.

She moved away without acknowledging his greeting.

"Please, Shira," he said, a step behind. "May I see you?"

"You've seen me already."

"I must talk to you."

"Talk to the wind. It will tell you all I have to say to you."

"Can you not spare me a moment?"

"Can you return the breath of life to my son?"

"You know I can't. If I could I would, for a terrible battle rages inside me."

"When you have won the battle, perhaps then we can talk."

"Shira, please."

"No!" She increased her pace. "You are a Roman, and I don't associate with Romans."

"I'm a Jew!" he protested.

"A Jew you were born, but a Roman you have become."

"No!"

"Yes!" She stopped and faced him, her eyes flashing

undisguised rage."You dress like a Roman," she fumed."You look like a Roman, and you think like a Roman. When you no longer act like a Roman, perhaps then you will be a Jew."

"As you wi–"

"Do not say as you wish to me! Never again say as you wish to me!"

Romulo turned on a heel and walked away.

"Romulo."

Why she uttered that word she did not know, and no sooner had it slid off her tongue than she wished she could call it back. Still, for some reason she could not explain, she was strangely drawn to this Jew/Roman who had shed his arrogance, humbling himself before her, seeking forgiveness for the heinous task that had been forced upon him. Harboring contempt for his despicable deed, and loathing for everything his uniform signified, still, in her heart dwelt an odd sense of compassion for this man who had come seeking her forgiveness.

Turning about, he met her gaze. "Yes?" he said.

"You once told me of a possible revolt," she said.

The anger in her voice had given way to calm, and Romulo felt the relief of a condemned man gasping for one more breath.

"The revolutionary forces are gaining strength," he said. "Some of my comrades talk of joining the rebels."

"And you?"

"If the movement develops, I will be a part of it."

"Is it wise that you tell me this?"

"I know you will speak of it to no one." He accepted her nod of assent. "Of course, I would have to resign my commission before involving myself with the rebels."

"It is said that death alone releases you from the Roman legion."

"There are ways. If they fail, I will still join the protest."

"God go with you."

"And with you." He left her with a cordial nod, assuring himself that they would meet again. Had she not said, "Never again say as you wish to me?"

Shira watched him go, having noted the anguish in his eyes, the sorrow in his voice. Still, he was a part of the Roman machine that destroyed whatever stood in its path. She wanted to hate him as much as she hated it, but she could not. Disquieted by an impulse to call him back, her lips parted, but no words came.

Three days later, reports of desertions from the Roman contingent in Jerusalem flew with the wind across Judea. Herod, incensed by what he proclaimed "an insult to the emperor," launched an immediate search for the deserters."Not one traitor shall remain alive!" he vowed.

Patrols were dispatched throughout the land to hunt down the deserters, and within days the road from Jerusalem to Jericho was lined with crosses bearing the slumping bodies of recaptured Roman legionaries.

Captain Romulo de Vincius's body was not among them.

***

Far removed from the craggy hills of the Judean wilderness, Crassus, chief magistrate of the Roman Senate, assumed his position at the podium facing the representatives. Slick, straight, gray hair swept his shoulders. With piercing black eyes he surveyed the gathering of consuls, meeting the gaze of every man, knowing well how each of them would vote on the matter he would soon bring before them. Assured that all was in order, he pounded the gavel.

"All rise," he said, "as we welcome our revered emperor, Augustus Caesar, by whose royal presence this body is highly honored."

Caesar, still a striking presence in his advanced years, strode briskly to the leather-bound throne on the dais. His chiseled features and stately manner evinced the strength and authority with which he ruled the world.

"You may proceed," said he in a strong voice. Sinking into the throne, he motioned the senators to resume their seats.

"With due respect, my lord," said Crassus, "your humble servant begs leave to address the emperor."

"Speak on, Crassus," said Caesar. "We all know of your store of words, and your penchant for using them."

A chuckle circled the Senate chamber.

"If it pleases my lord," Crassus said, "it has come to the attention of this body that there is mounting unrest in the province of Palestine."

"Well, it does not please your lord," the emperor said with a tinge of impatience, "but there has always been unrest in the province of Palestine. Is this the emergency for which you summoned me here?"

"We would not presume upon your grace," said Crassus, "except that it is agreed that the time has come for greater supervisory measures in the provinces, especially in Judea where uprisings have become increasingly frequent and more threatening to the empire."

"Threatening to the empire?" was the emperor's incredulous response."The empire is threatened by Judea?"

"Actually, my lord, there is a question of whether King Herod, in his present–condition–will be able for much longer to maintain order there."

"You mean Herod is no longer capable of ensuring the peace?"

"What I am saying, sire, is that Herod's methods of ensuring the peace have become antiquated. Brutality is no longer believed the best solution for discontent."

"Really?" said the monarch with the hint of a smile. "Would you have dared tell that to Antony or Pompey?"

"Forgive me, my lord, but we live in a modern age in which reason poses the need to displace violence. Negotiation and compromise are deemed more effective than the sword."

"Do you question Herod's loyalty?"

"Not his loyalty, sire," said Crassus, warming to the subject. "King Herod has served the empire long and faithfully. Our sources, however, report that he is losing control of the military, which hampers his ability to quell insurrection."

In the back of the chamber rose Dominius, a slender, sallow-faced young man, a new member of the Senate, whose late father once occupied his chair.

"If it please, my lord," said Dominius with a supercilious air, "are we not devoting an inordinate amount of time to discussion of an insignificant province that represents no more than a gnat on the backside of the empire?"

"A gnat it may be," countered his neighbor Cleotus, "but Judea has for many years been a viable source of revenue, and we have King Herod to thank for that."

"Herod!" scoffed his neighbor Miletus, an aging conservative who rarely spoke but now felt the need to be heard. "Yes, Herod has served long and faithfully no matter who ruled the empire, a chameleon whose allegiance is as pliable as chaff in the wind. A butcher who swam to power on a river of bloodshed by his own people. Rome owes Herod nothing!"

"Hear, hear," others murmured.

"What then do you propose, Miletus?" said Caesar.

"Send a delegation to Judea, my lord, that we may learn firsthand what conditions prevail there. Appraise Herod's reign, his methods, his purposes. If they are unacceptable on any account, strip him of authority, and banish him from the throne of Judea!"

Miletus's proposal generated a stir among the elders,

some in opposition, others in support. Crassus pounded his gavel for order.

Caesar's response was a contemplative nod, lending credence to the words of the aging Miletus.

"We must also remember," said Crassus, "that Judea is our line of defense against the Parthians to the east, as well as our access to Egypt. To allow interruption of that access at this time would be extremely unwise."

"Is this the opinion of the Senate?" said Caesar.

No vote was called for, but the vocal response was sufficient for the emperor to make his decision."Very well then," said he, rising. "A delegation it shall be."

"With your approval, my lord," said Crassus, "I will appoint a—"

"On the contrary," said Caesar on his way to the exit. "I haven't seen Egypt since Actium." He paused, allowing a moment of recollection for those who may have forgotten his defeat of Antony and Cleopatra at Actium thirty-five years before. "I myself shall journey to Egypt," said Augustus, "and pay a visit to my friend Herod in Jerusalem on the way. I'll be leaving as soon as arrangements are complete."

At the exit he paused and faced the astonished legislators. "If there is one among you," he said, "who would scoff at an old man who assigns himself such a task, be assured that this old man shall return." With a nod toward the throne from which he had just risen, he said, "And when I do, I will remove from that seat any man who dares occupy it while I'm gone."

So saying, the emperor departed, leaving the chamber in stunned silence.

"Judea?" Crassus muttered, incredulous. "Caesar in Judea?"

CHAPTER 4

"At the ready!"

Half a hundred rebels poised along the edge of the cliff awaited Romulo's command.

"Heave!" he shouted, and an avalanche of boulders tumbled off the cliff onto a supply train crawling through the narrow defile below. The Roman escort, donkeys, camels, and cart handlers were thrown into a frenzy. The Roman guards tried to escape, but the screaming rebels, brandishing swords, swarmed over the fleeing legionaries. Great was the clash of metal on metal. Moans of the wounded and angry curses of the combatants filled the air.

When it was over, the escort of Roman guards lay dead. With a warning to do no more business with the pagans from Italy, animal tenders and traders were allowed to go free.

In the beginning Dionysus had said, "If we feed the children, their fathers will come."

Such rebel raids on caravans bound for delivery to the Romans provided supplies that fed the children.

Confirming the Greek's prophecy, their fathers, indeed, had struggled up the slopes and across the gullies to join the ranks of the patriots. They came because they hated the Romans' domination of their beloved homeland, and detested Herod's brutal treatment of their countrymen. They came to escape political persecution and the burden of taxes levied by Herod and the Roman occupiers. Among those who sought to join the rebels were former slaves, even tax collectors stripped of their authority. Farmers, shepherds, and shopkeepers risked the hazards of the rugged wilderness to become a part of the Judean resistance.

Romulo was a man of whom they had heard, of whom they knew little, except for reports of his leadership, and his dedication to freedom for the people of Judea. Leading the revolt against tyranny, Romulo gave them reason to risk their lives, joining his fight to throw off the shackles of the Roman occupation.

Viewing his raw recruits with a critical eye, Romulo mused, "These, then, are those upon whose shoulders rests the future of Judea."

One who came was a bright young man named Zacheas, a former student whom Romulo chose as his personal orderly. Stockily built with a sparse beard, Zacheas was pleased to be so recognized, eager to do the bidding of the man he served. A tempestuous son of Judea, Zacheas resented with a fiery passion the pagan interlopers, longing for action against them.

"You must learn to control your emotions, Zacheas," Romulo advised.

"Control, yes," said Zacheas, "but, when I see our people being shackled by the Romans, and herded like sheep, I feel the need to explode."

"Think always with a clear head and an open mind, my young friend. The rain does not fall on the same vineyard every day. Our day will come."

***

It was in the spring that their day came. The men had grumbled through the harsh winter, surviving on meager provisions, wondering at times why they had been foolish enough to give up the warmth and comfort of their homes and families for the uncertainty of the Judean rebellion. Some questioned whether the freedom they sought was worth the sacrifice they were called upon to make. Even so, they had submitted to a rigid training regimen that Romulo assured them would mold them into "a fighting force of which Judea will be proud."

The morning broke cool and clear. Romulo, stoking the campfire, pondered whether his army was prepared to withstand the rigors of battle. He had praised his men, pleased with their progress. Still, the question remained: Was the fighting force that he had forged from raw Judean humanity capable of defending itself against the might of the Roman legion? The answer would come once they were urged into battle by the blast of the ram's horn.

Bolstered by his knowledge of the Romans' methods of defense, Romulo recalled that Augustus deemed it necessary to maintain only a limited force in Judea. After all, what uprising in tiny Judea could not be put down by a handful of well-trained, well-armed Roman soldiers with full stomachs?

"The men are ready, Romulo." It was Varisias, waiting at the door of the tent. He stepped aside, and Romulo led the way out.

From Zacheas Romulo took the reins of his stallion, and climbed into the saddle. Surveying the sea of anxious faces, all eyes were focused on him. In eerie silence, no one moved, and no one spoke. It was as though the world had come to a halt, waiting. Waiting, as if expecting Romulo to reveal some miraculous strategy by which they would be able to destroy the Roman nemesis plaguing their land.

Though some were apprehensive about going into battle, fever for action ran high.

"Are you ready?" Romulo shouted.

From the throats of the eager warriors burst a torrent of cheers. "Hail to him who was once a Roman!" called a voice from the midst of the crowd. Uplifted arms and clinched fists signaled approval.

"Yes!" Romulo responded. "I was once one of them, and proud I was to be a Roman soldier. But, no longer am I proud, except that, while I was once a Roman, I have always been a Jew!"

Shouts of eagerness bounced off the Judean hills, the level of excitement rising to a deafening pitch.

"We need have no fear of the Romans," Romulo said. "They are many and they are mighty, but we will hit them in the hills and in the villages, in the streets and in the marketplace when they least expect it. Their guards and patrols we will run through. We will destroy their supply trains and caravans, put the torch to their outposts, and we will not rest until Judea is free of the Godless pagans! Are you with me?"

To a man, the warriors had shouted, "Lead on, Romulo!"

Romulo's defensive strategy included destroying Roman sources of supply. "If they can't eat, they can't fight." Such was the case of a small caravan emerging from a cloud of billowing dust. From a peak above the cut in the mountain, Romulo watched the approach of five camels swaying under the weight of bundles of provisions lashed to their sides. Following the camels, a half dozen sure-footed, heavy-laden donkeys struggled up the steep incline. Behind the donkeys creaked ox carts piled high with supplies bound for the Roman contingent in Jerusalem.

At Romulo's side, Varisias said, "It's not much of a caravan."

"No," said Romulo, "but they carry supplies for the

Romans. Otherwise, the Roman guards would not be escorting them." He took another look. "How many Romans do you count?" he said.

"One in front, three in the middle, and four bringing up the rear."

"Is the Greek ready?"

Varisias did not meet Romulo's gaze. "The Greek is always ready," Varisias said. "He and his men relish these clashes."

Romulo cast him a questioning look.

"Sometimes," said the centurion, "I wonder if he enjoys them too much."

They turned their attention back to the pack train crawling through the mountain pass, men and animals in single file. The opening was scarcely wide enough for the loaded carts to squeeze through.

Romulo waited for the four rear guards on horseback to clear the entrance. "Now!" he shouted.

The rebels, with blood-curdling screams, catapulted off the cliff and onto the supply train below. Romulo launched himself onto the lead Roman guard, knocked him off his mount, and finished him with a dagger thrust to the throat. Agile as eagles his comrades attacked the Roman escorts, slashing with sword and lance. With a fierce exchange of blows, punctuated with cries of pain, and the shrill screams of frantic donkeys, horses and camels, the affray was soon over. Splotches of blood stained the dusty earth. The Roman escort was destroyed, and the traders, allowed to go free, were warned to deal no more with the Romans.

The rebels rounded up horses, pack animals and ox carts, and rushed them toward the sanctuary of the Judean hills.

"Romulo!" said the Greek with a broad smile."Some caper, eh?"

"Some caper, Dionysus. Your men handled it well."

"Aye, good men all. They are not sickened by the sight

of blood."

"Whose blood, Dionysus?"

"Whose– Is there a difference?"

"Our fight is with Rome, not Judea."

The Greek's smile disappeared. Eyes narrowed, voice defiant."Could be you worry too much, my friend," he said.

"Could be, but from now on the traders' blood shall remain their own."

For a moment their eyes met. After a tense moment, in which Romulo thought the

Greek might challenge his authority, Dionysus stalked away to join his friends.

Romulo watched him go. Would he one day be forced to bring the tempestuous Greek to heel?

Reports of rebel victories swept the land, with the hope of relief from Roman oppression. Now, there was Jewish opposition to be reckoned with. Now, the pagan interlopers could no longer ride roughshod over the land and its people. No longer would Judeans be intimidated into humbly stepping aside, lowering their eyes and bowing their heads when meeting temple priests in the marketplace. Now they could hold their heads high, defying the priesthood's apathy toward the rebels' efforts to drive the Romans from their beloved homeland.

Shira bas Haran welcomed the news of the patriots' successes. With secret wonder, she recalled the man whose name was whispered about as the heroic leader of the freedom fighters. Romulo. The Jew/Roman, recollections of whom had disturbed her slumber. Nightmares drenched her trembling body as she relived time after horrifying time the day Jabal was taken from her. In her dream, when the Roman guard snatched up her son and hauled him away, her terrified outcries shattered the unfeeling darkness.

She had recognized Antillus, who read her the king's terrifying decree. Times when Romulo appeared in her vision, he reached out to her, drew her to him, soothing her sorrow. Once, she woke with a start, perplexed that she had called out to him. She considered seeking Rabbi Josef's interpretation of the dream. In the end, though, she put the notion aside, unwilling to admit, even to herself, that the animosity she felt toward him who robbed her of her son had begun to wane.

Trudging up the hill to the marketplace, Shira reflected sadly that only the common folk of Judea respected the efforts of the revolutionary forces. Scoffing at the complacency of authorities who lent the patriots no support, she condemned the politicians and government officials who had grown wealthy dealing with the Romans. Especially was her caustic criticism aimed at the Sadducees, the worst offenders, who benefited most from the Roman occupation. Deploring what life in Judea would be like without the Romans, the Sadducees dared not risk the loss of luxury and privilege to which they had become accustomed. The supercilious Sadducees Shira detested almost as much as the pagan interlopers because they renounced the rebels as a collection of rabble who, themselves, should have been banished from Judea. Even the conservative Pharisees, deriding the patriots' opposition, contended that the patriots' protests would lead only to the devastation of Judea.

"What can you do, Shira?" Hannah had said when Shira spoke out against the arrogant temple priests and the hated Romans. "The authorities don't look kindly upon a woman who doesn't abide by the old ways."

"Then, who will do it, Hannah? What man among them will assert himself and demand recognition of the patriots? Those men out there in the hills are fighting to save Judea from the Roman vultures. How can they win without the support of the Council?" She paused, turning that thought over in her mind."I'll go there myself if it comes to that."

"To the Council?"

"Directly to Hillel if need be."

"The Council president!"

"I've heard him speak in the temple. Hillel is a good and reasonable man whose allegiance is to Judea, not Rome. Perhaps I'll first approach Rabbi Josef. If he thinks it's the right thing to do, then I'll do it."

"And if he doesn't think it is the right thing?"

With a confident toss of her head, Shira said, "I'll do it anyway."

"Why am I not surprised that you would not stop with Rabbi Josef?"

"Sometimes, Hannah, a woman speaks loudest when she speaks not at all, but now is not the time for silence."

Having outlined her plan to the rabbi, she was pleased that he favored her wish to appear before the Council.

"You deserve to be heard," the old rabbi said, "though the Council has many matters to consider, and we are not all of the same mind. However, I shall convey to the president your desire to appear before the Council. If he deems your cause worthy–"

"Worthy, rabbi? What is more worthy than the cause of Judea?"

"The cause of Judea, of course. But, as I have said, we are not all of the same mind. We must remember that there are those–in and outside the Council–who favor conditions as they now are. Supporting a movement against the Roman regime– To some that would cause much distress."

"Perhaps that's why we have become a nation of slaves."

"Slaves, my dear?"

"That's what my father believed. Have we not humbled ourselves in the presence of the enemy, he would say, and sacrificed our freedom for silver and gold?"

"Not all, Shira. Truly, some have, but not all."

"My father believed that God did not choose us to be laden like asses. He believed that any man who will not fight for freedom has no right to it."

"A brilliant man was Haran ben Saul. Would that he were here now to lend his fire and wisdom to our cause."

"He often said the pockets of our leaders are heavy with the pagans' gold, and our leaders no longer have the desire to resist."

"We are bidden not to judge, dear daughter, lest we ourselves be judged. The leaders, yes. Many have grown wealthy trading with the Romans, but the foundation of Judea is still our God, and our strength is still his covenant. That has not changed, and it will not change as long as there are Jews upon the earth."

The kindly old teacher took both her hands in his. "Do not give up on us, Shira," he said. "Judea needs you. It needs your spirit, and your devotion to the cause of freedom. In the end, the victory will be ours, but we must be patient." With a sad smile, he patted her hand, and said, "This is one of the privileges of old age. I can hold your hand without being admonished for it."

"Oh, Rabbi Josef," she cried, throwing her arms around him."You are so wise. Where would I turn without you?"

Taking his leave, he bade her be patient."I will talk with Hillel," he said, "and I believe that he will recognize that the cause of the resisters is also the cause of Judea."

With the hope of the rabbi's promise, Shira turned into the street lined with shops and booths. The odor of sweating human bodies, the stench of camel dung and over ripe fruit hung heavy on the sultry air. Elbowing her way past hawkers, she waved off the entreaties of sellers of fine Persian carpets, brocades, inlaid furniture, threads of silver and gold, squeezing through the mass of shoppers at the street side booths piled high with bright colored fabrics.

She could not know that when next she saw her dear friend Josef he would die in her arms.

CHAPTER 5

To conceal a royal guard of cavalry and a contingent of foot soldiers would have exceeded the imagination of Augustus Caesar's ablest magicians. It was no secret, therefore, that the emperor had landed at Joppa on the banks of the Mediterranean. Only one day after ships bearing the emperor and his military escort dropped anchor at Joppa, traders friendly to the rebels relayed to Romulo the news of their arrival, and the monarch's journey to Jerusalem had begun.

Like a gigantic serpent, the Roman entourage crawled across the plains past the caves of Beth-horon, emerging from the hills into the lowlands, and finally into view of the rebel lookouts.

Romulo had dispatched Dionysus and his men to observe the emperor's progress. At sight of the winding column, Dionysus wheeled his bay about and raced to where Romulo waited atop a mountain crest.

"He's coming, Romulo!" Dionysus shouted, skidding his horse to a stop. Eyes flashing, voice charged with excitement, the Greek leaped to the ground. "Can you believe it? Caesar's army right under our noses!"

Snaking through the cut in the mountain, the Roman ranks narrowed to a slender column, flaunting the military might that brought the world to its knees. At the head of the column rode Caesar himself who, despite the hot, wearisome trek overland from Joppa, sat straight as a dart aboard his black, sweat-slick Arabian stallion.

This was not the first time Augustus had visited Judea. In the year 37, after Herod annihilated the army of Antigonous, Augustus and Marc Antony came to bear official witness to Herod's ascension to the throne in Jerusalem. Before that time, Augustus had regarded Judea as little more than a hand-sized plot of earth bordering Egypt on the north. But, under Herod's rule, Judea had become a viable source of revenue for the coffers of Rome.

Even so, observing the dry, stony hills his army trod, Augustus mused with wonder that Crassus's appraisal of Herod's reign might have been accurate. How, except by force, could the king have extracted from the Judean desert the thousands of talents in tribute and taxes with which he plied Rome's ravenous appetite?

From the limestone peak overlooking the desert, Romulo watched the emperor's entourage squeeze through the defile. At one point Caesar passed directly below where Romulo stood. He could have leaped from the cliff, knocked the emperor off his black Arabian, slitting his throat with a dagger's flash. Wisely, he resisted the temptation to do so.

"When, Romulo?" said the Greek, his darting eyes aflame with anticipation of a fight.

"When?" Romulo said.

"When do we strike? My men and I—"

"We do not strike, Dionysus."

"Not strike!"

"To attack Caesar's elite guard would be pure folly. A

mouse's chances against a cobra would be better. You and your men will have to wait for another time."

"Wait?" The Greek was incensed."There may not be another time! All these months we've been getting ready for this. Caesar and his army–"

"They would cut us to pieces and feed us to their dogs, and all Judea would go up in flames."

"But Caesar–" Dionysus pleaded, eager for action.

Romulo pinned him with a steady gaze. "The taste of blood seems to have whetted your appetite for more," he said.

"Meaning?"

"You are no longer the man whose revulsion of tyranny gave him the courage to desert the legion."

Dionysus leered about, seeking support from his friends."Am I not now?" he sneered.

"I once respected you as a friend," Romulo said, "determined as I to destroy the enemies of freedom. But now, you wish only to destroy, even some of those we came to save. In the forces of freedom, there is no place for men who kill for the joy of watching other men die."

The Greek bared his teeth in a malicious grin. Leaping from his mount, he spread his arms, signaling those about him to give way. "Methinks our leader has grown soft," he snarled. "Perhaps what we need is a new leader, a man with the grit to stand fast and not tuck tail and run in the face of the mighty, eh, Romulo? A man who does not quake in the presence of the tyrant." He seized the dagger at his side and waved it with a threatening motion toward Romulo.

His challenge was answered with a flash of Romulo's short sword.

"Is it the emperor who still commands your allegiance," Dionysus chided, "stuffing your guts with fear of the cross? Eh, Romulo?"

The circle of spectators widened, and the Greek extended his long arms in a wing-like manner. Hunching forward, he lunged at Romulo, but Romulo sidestepped the thrust. Again the Greek swung his blade and missed. Romulo's quick jab slashed Dionysus's wrist, leaving a bloody gash.

Shocked at sight of his own blood, the Greek winced, his eyes narrowing to slits. His thick lips contorted into an angry scowl as he clutched the blade in both hands for a deadly strike. Flying at Romulo with an animal shriek, he flailed away with aimless swipes. Eluding the knife, Romulo lost his footing on the loose gravel and tumbled down an incline, landing on his back. His weapon flew from his hand.

The Greek was on him in an instant with a vicious laugh, choking with one hand, the other pricking Romulo's throat with the tip of his dagger. Romulo grabbed the Greek's blade hand in both of his, at the same time forcing a knee into the Greek's mid-section. Straining with hands and knees, he shoved Dionysus aside. The Greek landed head first against a boulder, stunned by the blow.

Romulo scrambled to his feet, catching the glint of his sword in the dust near where the Greek fell. One quick bound and the knife was in his grasp.

The Greek shook his head clear, and struggled to his feet with a token lunge at Romulo. Romulo, anticipating the move, countered with a swift thrust of the blade to the throat of the staggering Greek. Dionysus's mouth flew open. Lips twisted in shock, blood spurting from the gash in his throat, he plopped face dawn on the rocky soil, groaned once, and died.

Romulo surveyed the circle of silent faces, expecting the Greek's friends to assume the fight, but no one moved.

"You have the choice of staying or going," Romulo said in a loud voice. "If you would go, go now. If you choose to stay, you'll prove your dedication to the cause of freedom."

Some friends of the Greek sheepishly lowered their

heads, but stayed where they were.

Satisfied that the matter was settled, Romulo sheathed his sword. "Varisias!" he called.

"Here, Romulo."

In the eyes of his friend the centurion noted the pain of having taken the life of a comrade who once was a trusted ally. Almost, Varisias reached out to lay a comforting hand on Romulo's shoulder, then did not. A tacit look passed between them, each reading the thoughts of the other.

"See after the Greek for me," Romulo said, "then get the men mounted and back to camp. Keep them alert. With Caesar here, there's no telling what Herod might do to make himself look capable." Mounting the gray stallion, he said, "I'm going up to Jerusalem."

Varisias nodded and turned away, shouting orders to the men.

"Zacheas!" Romulo said.

"Here, sir," said the young orderly, leaping to his side.

"I'll be away for a day or two, Zacheas. Varisias will be in command. Do what you can to assist him."

"Varisias?"

"Yes."

"Have I not served you well, sir?"

"You have served me well," said Romulo, noting the look of disappointment on the face of his young aide that Varisias, instead of himself, had been appointed to lead in Romulo's absence.

"Then, why, sir? Why Varisias? Am I not worthy of your trust while you are away?"

The lad's troubled expression caused Romulo to wonder what had led him to such brashness. Surely, even prompted by youthful ambition, Zacheas must have known that his limited experience had not prepared him to displace the seasoned Varisias who was twice his age.

Learning that Zacheas's parents had perished when their home was destroyed by fire, Romulo had taken a special interest in the boy, caring for him as he might have cared for a son of his own. Still, he had never seen his young orderly display such angst. Was it jealousy he saw etched on his face? Jealousy of Varisias who had been a Roman officer for more years than Zacheas had lived?

For a silent moment, Romulo scanned the cloudless sky as if expecting to find there the answers he sought. To Zacheas, he said, "Before you can lead, you must first learn to follow. Stay close to Varisias, and you will learn well."

At rigid attention, Zacheas snapped a brusque salute. "May I go now, sir?" he said.

With a casual nod, Romulo returned his salute. "You may go now."

He watched the young rebel march briskly away without a backward glance.

Reining the gray about, Romulo dismissed the episode as an attempt by Zacheas to assert his youthful zealous nature.

From a distance, Varisias had observed the boy's immature behavior. Shaking his head with a wry grin, he returned his attention to the troops.

Romulo urged the stallion down the mountainside. His goal was to reach Jerusalem before Caesar arrived there. Even so, he could not dismiss the reality that in a corner of his mind dwelt thoughts of Bethlehem and Shira bas Haran.

**

Outside the walls of Jerusalem, Caesar raised his right hand, signaling his entourage to a halt. Peering beyond the walls, he was astonished by the beauty of the city revered by the Judeans as holy. Had Herod been responsible for this magnificent creation? If so, how could he chastise the king in the face of such splendor?

Herod's palace, rivaling the shrines of Egypt in stature and brilliance, stood near the south wall. Beyond the palace, vaulting above its neighbors, rose the glistening silver and gold temple. In his invasion of 64, Roman General Pompey destroyed the temple, but Herod, in a fruitless effort to placate the irascible Jews, had caused it to be rebuilt. Dominating the eastern sector of the Temple Mount loomed a white stone edifice, sumptuous in structure with an eighty-foot tower mounted on each of its four corners.

"That's the Antonia, sire," said the officer at Caesar's side. "The king's tribute to Marcus Antonius."

The emperor could hardly suppress a wry smile."Herod has always known where the power lay," he said. Augustus knew well Herod's penchant for adapting his allegiance to whoever occupied the throne in Rome. Still, despite Crassus's appraisal, for more than thirty years Herod had maintained order in Judea, reason enough for Caesar to support the vassal king. Though the emperor lauded Herod's accomplishments, Crassus's appeal was still worthy of his consideration.

"We live in a modern age," Crassus had said, "in which reason poses the need to displace violence." Time and circumstance are subject to change, Caesar pondered, but to bring a captive nation to heel, what competent military strategist would yield to reason over might?

The trek over rough desert hills from Joppa had been wearisome for men and animals. Tempers were strained, tension hanging heavy on the autumn air. A few days' pause at Jerusalem, Caesar reasoned, would delay his journey to Alexandria but little, and his troops would benefit from the respite. And his anticipated visit with Herod would help determine whether words, indeed, were stronger than the sword.

Astride his black stallion, Caesar led his steel-helmeted escort across the Kidron Valley to the gates of Jerusalem. Welcomed there by King Herod's guard, the king himself, in regal garb, now old–older than Caesar, haggard in his waning years–rode at the head of his mounted guard.

The two leaders exchanged greetings, after which the Romans pitched camp outside the walls of the city. An escort of Caesar's cavalry and foot followed Herod's guard into the streets of Jerusalem. In the company of his benefactor, King Herod beamed with pride, decked out in attire denoting his official stature, a rarity in recent years because of his declining health.

The entourage clopped along broad avenues to the king's palace. Anticipating Caesar's arrival, Herod had envisioned throngs of worshipful Judeans lining the parade route, scrambling for position along the streets, bowing low, humbling themselves, displaying their respect for the ruler of the world.

He was disappointed. Only minutes before, the air had been rife with the shouts of merchants and traders, donkey and camel handlers urging their charges toward the marketplace. But Caesar's arrival elicited little more than vague curiosity, squinting, suspicious eyes, and stony silence.

The seething Herod looked neither right nor left, incensed by the apathetic reception with which his Roman master was greeted. Taking shape already in the mind of the spurious king was a plot for retribution against his ungrateful subjects.

Approaching the palace gates, Caesar observed with wonder the mass of stolid faces on the parade route. No adulation nor joy did he see, and the only sounds were those of iron-shod steeds, creaking metal armor, and the pounding of hob-nailed Roman boots on the cobblestone street.

Romulo de Vincius watched with interest from the street side, in peasant garb, blending with the masses of brown-clad onlookers. Caesar rode past a dagger's length from where Romulo stood. For an instant their eyes met, the emperor cast him a quizzical half smile, then rode on.

Trumpets blared, drums rolled, and palace guards stood at stiff-legged attention as the world's most powerful man led his entourage into the palace compound, disappearing beyond the gates clanging shut behind them.

On the streets of Jerusalem, life again became a bustling mass, the emperor's arrival having stirred little more than idle wonder that he had come.

Romulo resented the haughty assurance that he saw in the eyes of Augustus Caesar. But it was the tyrant king who rode beside him whom Romulo most detested. Rome could be dealt with, requiring of its conquered nations only peace and tribute. For the insulting slight of the king's Roman idol, however, Romulo feared the vengeful Herod would pierce the heart of Judea with even more denigrating regulations. Briefly, he reflected on the prophecy of the stranger who had fallen in beside him at the theater exit: "The fear is that Judea may suffer even more restrictions imposed by the mad king."

CHAPTER 6

Approaching the marketplace, Shira was struck by a cacophony of angry voices and pounding hob-nailed boots. Always there were running, pounding boots, portending anxiety and fear, often tragedy.

Major Cassio on horseback shouted orders. Half a dozen legionaries scurried about, responding to his commands."Sergeant Quintas!" he barked.

"Sir!" said the burly legionary, pulling up beside him.

Cassio aimed his riding crop at a message scrawled in blood on the city wall: DEATH TO ROME! "Find out who is responsible for this outrage," Cassio screamed, "and bring him to me at once!"

"That won't be easy, sir," Quintas said. "These people don't take to cooperating with the authorities."

"I did not ask for an appraisal, sergeant!"

"No, sir!"

"Then do I as say. Round up these people, and let no one escape. Find the culprit and bring him to me!"

With a sharp salute, Quintas was off, yelling

instructions to the Roman soldiers with drawn daggers, herding together the defiant Judeans.

"Ten lashes to every man until one of them confesses!" Cassio screamed.

Quintas grabbed a man by the arm and held him while a comrade stripped him to the waist, tying his hands to a whipping post. The soldier began flailing away with his bone-tipped lash, opening bloody gashes on the victim's bare back. The man cried out, writhing in pain.

Shira watched in horror as the lash fell time after time, ripping the man's flesh with merciless blows. From somewhere in the crowd, Shira heard a small, familiar voice.

"A moment, sergeant," said the voice, hardly more than a whisper.

Searching the gathering, Shira's gaze fell upon Rabbi Josef.

"If you will," said the old teacher, calmly appealing to the Roman officer.

Cassio raised a hand. The whip, poised to strike again, hung suspended in the hand of Sergeant Quintas.

"What is it, old man?" Cassio barked.

"I am the one," said Josef, "who wrote on the wall."

Rabbi Josef! Shira was beside herself with anger, fearing for the life of her dear old friend. "No!" she protested. Shoving people aside, she tried to reach him. "Josef!" she cried, grasping the old rabbi's narrow shoulders. "Josef, no!"

"I must do this, Shira," he said in a low voice. "I must do this."

Puzzled though he was by the rabbi's confession, Cassio hesitated only briefly. "Out with him!" he commanded, and three soldiers laid hold of the aged man of God and dragged him to the whipping post.

Shira tugged at Josef's arm, trying to rescue her devoted friend from what she knew would be certain death, for his ancient body could not survive such a brutal lashing.

"No, please!" she cried, but a Roman soldier shoved her aside.

Josef's hands were lashed to the whipping post, and Quintas began wielding the thong, slashing his frail body.

Shira could only watch as Josef's bleeding body slumped in agonizing pain. One final blow caused his frail body to collapse. He had uttered not a sound. The Romans left him where he fell.

Shira rushed to Josef's side and freed his hands from the post. "Josef!" she cried, cradling his head in her arms."Dear, dear Josef, what have you done?"

"Judea," he whispered through trembling lips. "For Judea."

"You are no more guilty than I!"

"Weep not for me, Shira, but for Judea. In our own way, we are all guilty." With his last breath he gasped, "Hillel–it is arranged–you must–you must–"

"Josef! Josef!"

His ears closed in death; the old rabbi did not hear her frantic plea.

***

From the Dung Gate the narrow road leading south to Bethlehem overflowed with travelers. Some were pilgrims who traveled many miles on foot, some on lethargic donkeys, to worship at the temple in Jerusalem.

Shira was hardly aware of those around her, filled as she was with sorrow for Rabbi Josef, and with revulsion for the ruthless Romans who had beaten him to death. "Slaughtering old men and innocent children!" Shira fumed silently."Surely, this is not what God intended when he promised to take care of us."

Approaching the Bethlehem wall, she melted into the rush of people entering the village gate. Beyond the well she caught sight of a man standing apart, wearing a brown muslin cloak, his face hidden beneath the mantle that covered his head. She smiled. Drawing upon the intuitive magic with which women are blessed, and by which men are confounded, she knew the man waiting there was Romulo de Vincius.

The nightmares had occurred less frequently of late. Even so, stirring a pot of soup, grinding at the wheel, or gleaning in the fields, she found her thoughts drifting with disturbing frequency toward him whose name had become synonymous with the Judean rebellion. That she harbored some bewildering closeness to him she sought to deny, though puzzled that she feared for the safety of him whom she once abhorred. In the night, she sensed his nearness, confessing to a hollowness upon waking to find that he was not there.

She dared not allow herself to dwell on why her feeling for Romulo had evolved from hatred to a sense of admiration.

Her heart was nonetheless heavy with sadness for the death of Rabbi Josef, but she felt a lightness in her step that carried her toward the well. Quickening her pace, her lips silently formed the word, "Romulo."

As though having heard her call to him, he turned abruptly, his smile evincing his joy at seeing her again.

Shira looked neither right nor left as she approached the well, avoiding an encounter with friends who might call to her. She kept walking until she passed Romulo.

Following a step behind, he said, "Shira?"

At a safe distance from her friends at the well, she faced him.

"Romulo," she said.

"Shira!" His arms ached to reach out to her, to hold her, to share with her the joy of having her near."Tonight," he said. "May I come to you tonight?"

"Tonight, yes!" she said, casting aside in a moment of

joy the misgivings of the past.

He touched her hand, then quickly slipped away.

Watching him go, she swept her cheek with the hand he had touched, then hurried home, for soon Bethlehem would be swathed in darkness.

***

Up the ladder to the loft she had scampered, tossing aside her soiled robe as she went. With water from the cistern she laved her body, anointing her arms and legs with her favorite essence. She donned a pale blue robe, then brushed and bound her hair. On the way down the steps she heard his call.

Pausing a moment to catch her breath, Shira greeted him at the door.

"Peace be with you," she said.

"And with you." Tanned and smiling, Romulo stepped into the room.

Shira invited him to the table, and placed before him fresh barley bread and a basket of grapes, apples, and pomegranates.

"I hear much of your leadership," she said, pouring the wine.

"Leadership is the easy part," said he, sipping at his cup. "Judea is fortunate to have good men who are willing to fight for her freedom."

"You must know of Caesar's arrival," she said.

"Yes, I was there."

"You saw him?"

"He rode past me closer than you are. We watched his army cross the desert and through the pass. I lost a friend because I wouldn't give the order to attack."

"Attack Caesar?"

"We were greatly outnumbered. It would have been suicide for the rebels."

"Your friend–"

"The Greek, Dionysus. He challenged me, and left me no choice."

"I too lost a friend today," she said. "A dear old rabbi named Josef. Someone had scrawled an anti-Roman protest on the wall near the marketplace. A Roman officer ordered every man lashed until someone confessed. After the first man was beaten, Rabbi Josef told the officer he had written the message, death to Rome. 'For Judea,' he told me with his dying breath. Poor Josef. He couldn't have hurt anyone!"

Romulo covered her hand with his. "I'm sorry for your loss," he said, "but our fight is not with Rome only. Many of our own people don't believe in what we're trying to accomplish. Even the temple priests don't want anything to do with us."

"Rabbi Josef was not one of them. He strongly supported the revolution. He arranged for me to appear before the Council to seek their support."

"The Council?"

"Yes! Hillel will send word when it is arranged."

"Hillel?" Romulo said, pleased. "Meeting with the Council! No matter what they decide, my men will be encouraged that because of you they do not fight alone. With or without the Council's help, we must fight on. The Romans now know that we are not a bunch of bootlickers eager to do their bidding, nor sheep to be led to the slaughter."

She smiled. "You would have liked my father," she said. "He too stood up for what he believed, and died because of it."

"There are many who feel as your father did, but for fear of harm to their families, they take no stand." He paused briefly, then said, "I once heard a very wise man say that every man must assume his place in time, or sacrifice for nothing his soul. We must keep fighting, Shira, to rescue Judea from the clutches of the beast. Otherwise, we have no reason to fight."

She refilled their wine cups, and offered him a sweet cake. "And what is your reason, Romulo?"

Over the rim of his cup he studied her intense brown eyes, the flawless complexion, her full, tantalizing lips that stirred his emotions. He knew the answer. Many nights had he lain awake forming in his mind the words he would speak if he was ever asked that question. Even so, his response did not come easily.

"The Romans destroyed my father and mother, just as they did yours," he said, his voice a hoarse whisper. "Their homeland for many years has been held hostage by the pagans of Rome. And because of one vile order that I was compelled to obey, I have been denied the joy of the woman I love."

"Who?"

"You."

"Romulo!"

"Yes! Long before that tragic day of Herod's decree, I watched you in the marketplace and wanted to call to you. But I was a Roman then, and dared not insult your Jewish pride. In quarters at night I heard my comrades boast of their conquests, wishing I could tell them about Shira bas Haran, the most desirable of them all. But I could not tell them, because then I knew you only from what I had seen. I now know you for what I feel in my heart."

He reached out to her, and drew her to him, intoxicated by the warm softness of her body, the tantalizing aroma of her womanness.

For so long her devotion to Ezlon had denied her the freedom of emotional release. But now, in the arms of the man who had humbled himself before her, she felt herself being swept away in a torrent of desire. She returned his kisses, and together they lay in complete surrender.

They slept. Romulo's burden of guilt he felt melting

away.

Darkness gave way to the breaking day, and the lovers were wakened by the sound of a heavy fist pounding on Shira's door.

"Who is it?" she called.

The intruder identified himself. "Major Marcus Cassio of the Roman legion."

"Cassio!" Romulo said, bouncing to his feet. "I'll go."

"No," said Shira, donning a robe."I'll see what he wants."

Again the knock sounded.

"I'm coming," said she."You need not knock the door down." To Romulo she whispered, "The risk is too great. Out the back way with you, and over the rooftops. I will see to Major Cassio."

Romulo opened his mouth to protest, but she pressed a finger to his lips."Go now," she said. With a quick kiss, she left him and went to face the restless Roman.

She opened the door and said, "Yes? What is it you want?"

Cassio's face flared red with irritation.

Shira recognized him as the officer who ordered the beatings in the market place the day before. With Rabbi Josef's dying words fresh in her mind, she felt the need to lash out at this arrogant Roman, but caution stilled her tongue.

In his left hand Cassio held a rolled parchment, and with his right hand he flicked the riding crop against his knee. Behind him stood two legionaries at strict attention.

"May I come in?" said Cassio with a smirk.

Shira abhorred his condescending manner. Romans needed no consent nor invitation to enter her home. The major could have stormed her door and dragged her screaming into the street and she would have been powerless to resist.

Stepping aside, she watched Cassio's eyes scanning

her sparse furnishings. He moved to the door leading to the next room. Fearing that Romulo hadn't been able to escape in time, Shira could feel her heart pounding. The intrusive Roman turned away without comment, and she allowed herself to breathe again.

"Ah," said he with a mirthless grin, indicating the table. "A table set for two, and two wine cups. You have had a guest?"

"I have many guests."

"Yes, of course," he said, consulting the parchment. "You are called Shira?"

Fool! she wanted to scream. *You knew that before you came!* Instead, she said only, "I am Shira."

"It has come to the attention of the authorities that a man–a certain Romulo–has been known to frequent your home."

Frequent, indeed! she fumed inside."You have been misinformed, major."

"We have witnesses. Romulo has been seen coming here."

"He was here," she said, "on the day he and his murdering friends stole my baby and bashed his head against the village wall! Is that the Romulo you're looking for?"

Cassio smirked, "There is only one Romulo."

"If your mission is to find this–Romulo–you would do well to look elsewhere. If
he were here he would be dead."

"Dead?"was the major's haughty response. "Surely you–"

"Do not toy with me, major. This Romulo of yours killed my baby son because of Herod's insane decree. You can't be so naive as to believe that I would allow him to frequent' my home. Nor you, for that matter. Now if you will excuse me, I have work to do."

Cassio raised the whip as if to strike her, but did not.

Instead, he fondled a strand of her hair as a jeweler might appraise a precious gem.

"I will find your Romulo," he hissed, "and when I do—"

"And when you do, I hope he tears out your filthy heart and feeds it to your fellow swine!"

He struck her squarely on the mouth with the hand that a moment before caressed her hair. Shira fell against the wall, wiping blood from her face.

"You bloody bastard!" she screamed, diving headlong at the shocked Roman.

The guards caught her by the arms. Cassio, eluding her lunge, strode briskly to the door. The soldiers held the raging Shira until he was gone, then joined the departing major in the street.

Shira dropped to her knees, bowed to the floor, and wept."For this we wandered forty years in the wilderness!" she cried. "Almighty God of Abraham, Isaac, and Jacob, where are you now?"

CHAPTER 7

For twelve days and twelve nights rain drenched the land of Judea, eroding the spirit of Romulo's warriors camped in the wilderness. Soaked to the skin, he completed the changing of the guard, looking forward to the comfort of his tent.

A half hour's ride from where he sat his gray stallion stood a Roman outpost. He envied the legionaries their hot food, imported wine, and dry, warm beds which he once enjoyed as a Roman captain. He wished he could provide the same comforts for his men, volunteers who had left their homes, their wives and children, to join him in the fight for freedom.

"Hah!" he scoffed at the rain-heavy sky. "What have I to offer these who have come to sacrifice themselves in a war that only God could win?"

At the door of his tent he handed the reins to Zacheas. Inside, Varisias greeted him with a cup of hot chicken broth. Romulo accepted with thanks, and seated himself cross-legged by the fire.

"Zacheas set the fire," Varisias said. "And heated the broth, of which there is little left."

"A good lad, Zacheas. If his ambitions were a reality, this war would have been over long ago."

"How much longer can we hold out?"

Romulo cast him a sharp look."The Greek once asked me that. I said how long is forever? He laughed and went back to work."

"That's the Greek all right. You miss him, don't you?"

"I do."

"So do I."

Rain pelted the tent. Romulo removed his boots and placed them by the fire to dry.

"We were a good team," Varisias said. "The three of us."

Romulo held his wet feet to the flame."What are they saying?" he said.

"The men? Nothing."

"It would be better if they were at each others' throats. They're tired of fighting. So am I."

"But they won't give up."

"No. The stakes are too great. We've come too far to turn back now."

"This kind of weather gives them time to think about what they're missing back home."

"Do you want to go?" Romulo said.

"I'd be lying if I said I didn't. I haven't seen my son in seven years. I doubt he would recognize me now."

"Well, then, what's keeping you here?"

"Judea is not yet free. Until it is, nobody will go home." said Varisias. He took up a stick of wood, poked at the fire, tossed it onto the embers. "What about you, Romulo? I've never heard you speak of your family."

Shira bas Haran was not his family, but he had no other. Numerous nights had he spent with thoughts of her tumbling through his mind. Disrupting his slumber, also, was the matter of her appearance before the Council. Having heard no report of the elders' decision, Romulo pondered whether Shira had yet been summoned to the Council chamber.

"I have no family," he said.

With a silent nod, Varisias sipped at his broth."You asked about the men," he said."I must say I've heard some of them grumbling about whether we can win against the Roman legions. They question how long we can go on fighting."

"We must go on. No self-respecting Jew can abide losing." Romulo had long since stopped thinking of Varisias as a Roman."We have to believe we can win. Without our belief we're nothing. The Romans may conquer the rest of the world, but Judea they will never conquer. They can dominate us, they can trample us with their hob-nailed boots, but they will never own us!"

Varisias nodded in agreement. "They didn't do well against the Bedouin either."

"The Bedouin?"

"We just got word that a Roman detachment was routed by desert tribesmen led by a chieftain named Amrak. The Bedouin made off with more than fifty Roman horses."

"That's not surprising," said Romulo. "The desert people hate Rome as much as we do."

"Uh-huh," Varisias said. "Maybe that's what the men need."

"What's that?"

"Some action–to take their minds off home and family. They've been cooped up here for too long–like a huddle of wet hens."

"After the rains stop," Romulo said. "They'll see plenty of action after the rains stop."

In the back of his mind he filed away the name of the desert chieftain Amrak.

CHAPTER 8

A favorite endeavor of young Hebrew scribes and Sadducees was manning their booths in the market place, debating the interpretation of Scripture. The scribes, adhering to the teachings of the Pharisees, believed that life did not end at the grave. The Sadducees, however, contended that life after death was an empty myth, that the only hope for mankind was here and now, and that the salvation of Judea was passive acceptance of Roman domination.

Approaching the marketplace, Shira was attracted by loud voices, encountering a circle of bystanders observing the debate. The scribes were arguing that tenets of the Scriptures were the past, present, and future of Judea, and that Rome was the oppressor, not the savior of their land.

The Sadducees countered that without Rome there would be no Judea.

Shira tried without success to bridle her tongue. "What have the Romans done for us," she said, "except trample us underfoot?"

The circle of eyes abruptly swung to her, a new, unexpected voice. With contempt the debaters viewed her for so boldly interrupting their scholarly discussion. A priest lifted his chin and peered at her from the bottoms of his supercilious eyes. "And who, may I ask," said he with a condescending air, "are you to speak so?"

"I am a Judean," Shira said quietly. "I have the same right as you to speak."

The smirking priest faced his colleagues, scoffing with them at this peasant woman who had the audacity to disrupt their learned debate.

"And would you, miss–" With an arm he swept the gathering of his colleagues.

"–instruct us in the Scripture and the Law, not to mention the politics of life within the Roman empire?"

"The Romans are not welcome here," said Shira, "and Herod is a blood-thirsty despot, but the priests are the evil ones."

"Indeed!" derided the priest. "And by what authority do you propound such wisdom?"

"I make no claim to the piety which you display as a badge of wisdom and authority, demanding the respect of those you consider less worthy," she said. "It is not the Law of the Lord that breaks the backs of Judeans. The temple priests are the antagonists, with their man-made laws and assessments."

As she talked, the crowd grew larger, eyes focused on the young woman who had the courage to speak out. Soon she was surrounded by dozens of attentive bystanders.

"Do the priests pay taxes?" Shira went on. "God requires the tenth only. Who is it who demands the tributes and the temple tax?"

"It is the Law," said the priest significantly.

"Do not preach to me of the Law, priest. The Law says thou shalt not kill, yet my son was murdered by that maniac who occupies the throne. The Law says thou shalt not steal, but you priests rob us in the name of the Law."

Rankled by Shira's impertinence, the Sadducees, even so, dared not restrain her for fear of arousing protests among her sympathizers. "I, like you, was born a Jew," she went on. "I wear with pride the birthright that makes me a child of God. But, I abhor you and your kind, priest, you who find no reason nor the spine to fight to free God's people from the yoke of Roman oppression."

"You speak treason."

"I speak the truth! Do you fear the truth?"

"What do you, a simple peasant, know of truth?" Again he appealed to his colleagues, who nodded in solemn agreement.

"I have no regard for the authority which you so proudly display," Shira said, "demanding respect of any you believe unworthy. You're not the only ones endowed with wisdom." To the crowd, she said in a loud voice, "Is there no pride left in Judea? Have we yielded to the pagans who view us only with contempt?"

From the gathering rose cries of "Hear! Hear!"

Across the way, apart from Shira's audience, but within earshot, Major Cassio, flanked by half a dozen legionaries, listened casually, for such gatherings were permitted under supervision. To Sergeant Quintas at his side, Cassio said, "Who is this woman?"

"I don't know, sir," Quintas said. "Maybe a housemaid?"

"Find out," said the major, prompted by the notion that somewhere before he had seen this woman. "A housemaid I wager she is not."

Quintas turned aside as Shira's voice rose.

"I have not renounced God, as some would charge," she said. "I have only renounced those who would be God— with their laws and taxes and tyranny."

In the beginning the crowd had been apprehensive of Shira's fiery harangue. Then, as she challenged the arrogant priests, the onlookers applauded her. Caution taking flight, they responded with shouts of agreement and admiration for one of their own with the courage to challenge the hypocrisy of the priests, some with uplifted arms, others shaking defiant fists.

"It was not the Law of God that left me childless," Shira said. "And it is not God who tramples with heavy boots and bloody swords the hallowed ground of our father Abraham."

"Abraham himself paid tribute to God," said a priest weakly, "and adhered to the Law."

"You parade your piety in the marketplace," she shot back, "bidding us bow down before you, pausing as you walk by, paying you homage. You are not a man of God, but an informer, an enforcer of laws of your own making that burden the backs of the people. You priests care only for yourselves, and function only for each other."

As she talked, Quintas returned. To Cassio, he said, "All I could find out is that she's only a field worker, sir."

"Then she is not a threat to the empire?"

Quintas sniggered. "I think not, sir," he said, returning his attention to Shira.

"Is there no refuge from the laws of the priests?" Shira challenged the assembly."Is there no escape from the bondage of the dogs of Rome?"

Cassio had listened with little interest before, but now he bristled. "Dogs of Rome!"

To Quintas, Cassio said in a voice loudly enough for all to hear, "Sergeant, the activities of the Jews shall be curtailed immediately! They will not be permitted to congregate in the marketplace, and there will be no further public gatherings of local inhabitants in the city of Jerusalem. Not on this day, and not on any day until further notice! That is the order of the king!" Cassio stormed away.

The uneasy crowd fell silent.

Shira watched the major strut past, angrily slapping his

knee with the riding crop. Incensed by his arrogance, she shouted at his departing back, "May your bowels be inhabited by vipers!"

Abruptly Cassio turned and shot a finger in her direction. "Arrest that woman!" he demanded.

Cassio! Shira recognized him as the Roman officer who had pounded on her door in search of Romulo. Major Cassio, who had ordered the lashing of Rabbi Josef. She moved away in haste, seeking to escape arrest. Guards rushed to take her, but the crowd closed in, immersing her in a sea of brown muslin robes.

Caught up in the flow of the mob, Shira was startled by the sound of a man's voice at her side."Do not be alarmed," he said. He grasped her arm and guided her forward. "Keep looking straight ahead. If you turn to look, others will look also, and our lives could be in danger."

Aid from any source was welcome now. Shira did as she was told.

"You are Shira bas Haran?" the man said.

"I am."

"We must talk. I'll come to you tonight."

"How—you— How will you know where to find me?"

"I will find you," he said. "The beauty of such a lovely flower the darkness cannot hide." He steered her away from the crowd and into a narrow passageway. "You will be safe here," he said. "Go quickly."

Dashing away, she longed to see his face, but dared not look back.

***

Stewing around the house, Shira went about cleaning, scrubbing, grinding grain enough to last for days, doing things that didn't need doing. With a head full of puzzlement, she couldn't keep her mind off the man who rescued her at the market. Who was he, and why was he coming to her home without having been invited? Then it occurred to her–why should she care who he was or what he wanted–except that he had saved her from the hounds of Major Cassio? That was enough to keep her head buzzing.

Hardly had she lit the candle before she heard his knock at the door. The candle's flickering glow danced across the room, lighting her way. Greeting him at the door she saw a man whose voice she recognized,, but whose face she had not seen. The candle light fell on his deeply tanned face, high cheek bones, a broad smile, waiting for her to invite him in.

She stepped aside to let him pass, motioning him to the table, beside which he plopped down on a cushion, accepting her offer of wine.

"I hope you will forgive me for being so mysterious earlier," he said.

His accent told her he was not Judean. Galilean perhaps.

"There is no need for forgiveness," she said. "I thank you for rescuing me. I also must confess that I'm curious as to who you are, and why you are here."

"My friends call me Judah," he said. "Judah ben Hezekiah of Galilee."

She caught a quick breath. Here, sitting at her table, staring without shame into her eyes, was the legendary leader of the Galilean patriots!

"Oh!" she said. "I have heard of your heroism against the Romans."

Judah sipped at his wine cup. "You, and others like you," he said, "are the heroes who stand up for what you believe. I was struck by your words in the market place. It took great courage to speak so."

"I have no fear of the Romans. First they killed my father, and my mother died because of it. Then they murdered my son Jabal to satisfy the whim of the blood-thirsty Herod."

"I heard about that," said he. "I'm sorry for the loss of your son."

"There is nothing more they can take from me," she said, refilling their cups. "Tell me, Judah ben Hezekiah, why have you come to me?"

"Listening to you speak this afternoon, I knew you felt as I do, that we cannot be free until the shackles of Rome have been broken. The degradation of living under foreign control must end. That's why we Galileans continue to resist."

"In Judea also there is much unrest."

"Unrest is the mother of revolution. Still, there are some who are not willing to sacrifice for the freedom they long for."

"What you say is true, and yet there are others who believe as you do, who have the determination to resist."

"One of those," he said, "is why I am here."

She gave him a startled look.

"Romulo de Vincius," he said.

Apprehensive, she said, "How do you know Romulo?"

"Only by reputation. Although for generations animosity has simmered between Judea and Galilee, the news of heroism rides on the wind. Romulo de Vincius: Jew, Roman, deserter from the legion, leader of the Judean rebellion," Judah recited. "I must confess, Shira bas Haran, that, despite the joy of your company, it was my search for Romulo that led me here. We traced him to you."

Silently she observed the slender fingers holding his cup, pondering the purpose of Judah ben Hezekiah. His open frankness led her to believe that his quest was honorable. Even so, she must exercise caution, lest she say something that might jeopardize the safety of Romulo, and his fight to free Judea.

"Why have you come looking for Romulo?" she said.

"Have no fear," Judah said. "It's common knowledge that others seek him also, but for different reasons. Herod and the Romans want his head. I want only to offer my services, along with those of my men."

"I understand your opposition to the Romans, but Galileans and Judeans–fighting for each other?"

"Two thousand of my men are deployed in the hills of Judea, some in Samaria, and others along the Jordan. They can't all come here to testify on my behalf, but I assure you, Shira bas Haran, if my purposes were not honorable, I wouldn't risk death on a Roman cross by showing my face in Judea.

"The time has passed when we can afford to think of ourselves as Galileans and Judeans, but as Jews. Only together can we rid our land of the vassal king and his Roman masters.

"Romulo was once one of them. I would be honored to serve under his command, but I need your help to find him."

Shira's mind raced back to the day Jabal was taken from her. For that she had hated Romulo, but she could no longer hate him who had awakened in her emotions she had thought long dead. The man who even now invaded her dreams and confused her thinking. Before, she had detested him, but now she found the need to shelter him from harm.

In the eyes of Judah ben Hezekiah she perceived the same burning dedication to freedom by which Romulo was driven, convinced that through Judah's veins flowed the same dedication that enabled Romulo to challenge the Romans.

"Yes, Judah ben Hezekiah," she said, "I will help you find Romulo." Silently she prayed that what she was about to do would meet with the approval of God."I am unsure of his whereabouts at this time," she said finally. "I can tell you only where he was when I last knew."

CHAPTER 9

Shira's heartbeat quickened as she waited in the Council chamber, apart from the elders, uneasily folding and unfolding her hands on her lap. Three days ago, a young man showed up at her door and informed her in a toneless voice that the Council had agreed to grant her an audience. The day and time were arranged.

Many hours she spent rehearsing what she wanted to say to the Council. Time and again she rolled over in her mind what she wanted them to hear, until the words came almost unbidden, assuming a life of their own. And now the time had come to say them.

She took a deep, apprehensive breath as the aged leader, Hillel, rose to address the assembly of seventy sages. His bushy eyebrows hovering above dark, deep-set eyes, he studied their faces, recalling their political stances of the past. Advised in advance of Shira's purpose, he tried to anticipate their reaction to his pending proposal. Heavy as a millstone upon his heart lay the question: Could he in good conscience propose that the Council sanction resistance to Roman domination, possibly resulting in the destruction of his beloved Judea? Or should they continue to accept Roman occupation without resistance, a betrayal of their Jewish pride, and denial of their faith in God's covenant with the Fathers to deliver the enemy into the hands of Judea?

Now, here sat this young woman, Shira bas Haran, who had come to plead the cause of the rebels. What will she say? And how, if at all, will her pleadings influence the deliberations of the Council?

Rebel supporters were concerned about reported losses in recent clashes with the occupying troops. Hillel knew that. He had heard also that the patriots' supplies–chiefly the spoils of early encounters with Roman units–were rapidly being diminished. Their success or failure, and the future of Judea, might well hang in the balance of whatever action the Council decided to take.

Some Council members lauded the benefits of Roman rule, condemning the rebels' opposition as suicidal for Judea. When the time came for Shira to speak, therefore, those opposed to the patriots' resistance listened without emotion to her plea for food, clothing, and medical supplies, "that will let them know that they are not fighting alone."

Hillel had introduced her as the daughter of Haran ben Saul, "once a respected member of this body, who carried to the grave his pursuit of freedom for Judea."

"Your regard for me is but little," Shira had said, "for I have not been as faithful to the Scriptures as I might have been. And I have belittled you for your lack of concern for those who fight and die for our beloved country. Even so, you must agree that life under the heel of the detested Roman occupiers, whose emperor even now resides in the king's palace, can no longer be tolerated.

"I plead for your help, not only for those who every day risk their lives for the cause of freedom, but for our beloved Judea. My father, who once sat where you now sit, believed that God did not choose us to be laden like asses. He believed this land was given us by God himself, and that God can take it from us if we do not defend it against the Godless pagans."

Out of respect for her late father, the elders, some with heavy eyelids and strained patience, suffered the entreaties of this unlearned young woman, questioning why she had even been permitted to speak. Indeed, one of their number, Nicholais, responded by reviling any who would resist Roman domination.

"To accept Roman control is inevitable," Nicholais said in a weary tone. "We no longer have a choice. To resist is futile. Every other nation in the Roman empire has acquiesced and prospered. Continued revolt in Judea serves only to subject us to more strenuous control.

"We cannot afford, by sanctioning the efforts of these peasant deserters, who themselves should be banished from our land, to bring about its destruction. We cannot allow our women and children to be ravaged for the sake of dogma whose time has passed, and for dicta whose teeth have long since been dulled by the stones of circumstance.

"The sooner this Romulo—who, I understand, once fought as a Roman—the sooner he and his rabble are driven from the land, the sooner Judea will know peace and prosperity. The taste of defeat rarely touches the Roman palate, nor will it in Judea."

A blanket of silence fell over the chamber.

Nicholais resumed his seat, and looked to Hillel for a response. Shira glared at him, fighting the temptation to shout her objection to his inflammatory remarks.

Hillel rose, his eyes locked on those of the vitriolic Nicholais.

Ranged in a semicircle according to seniority sat the seventy judges. Facing them were the rabbinical members of the Council, beyond whom were seated the ushers, servants, beadles, and guards.

With a discerning eye, Hillel, physically eroded by age, but nonetheless mentally strong, scanned the hushed assembly, silently inviting response to Nicholais's invective.

There was none. Hillel interpreted their silence as agreement with Nicholais's sentiment. Bowing his bushy head in reverent thought, he folded his thin arms across his hollow chest. "It is believed by some that God has abandoned Judea," he said. "But, it is more likely that Judea has abandoned God."

An uneasy stir swept the chamber as the elders pondered Hillel's challenging charge.

"There is among us," the old scholar went on, "some who would desert the cause of Judea in favor of the pagans. They are the ones who profit from trade with the hated Pax Romana. And, though we deliberate now in private, before the fall of darkness upon our land, what we say here will reach the ears of the oppressors. That is the risk we take for being who we are, as opposed to the weaklings that they perceive us to be." He paused, peering with disapproving eyes, into the face of Nicholais.

Nicholais did not meet his gaze.

"You know who you are," Hillel continued, "just as we know who you are. Think not that our eyes are blind to your chicanery. Know, also, that God will punish you for betraying his people. Sadducees, Pharisees, scribes, rabbis, priests, laity–in the eyes of the Lord none is separate from the others. We are all Jews, raised from the seeds of Father Abraham, and as Jews, we must believe and act as one to preserve the sanctity of this holy land with which he has blessed us. We will all one day be judged according to what we do, not by what we say.

"We have listened, some with interest, some with sighs of intolerance, to the words of Shira bas Haran. Yes, at times she has been irreverent. Even so, her concern is not for herself, but for Judea. Hers was one of the innocents slaughtered by Herod in his insane attempt to destroy the male infants, determined to rid the land of the babe born in Bethlehem, by whom he feared being deposed. And so it is with good reason that Shira bas Haran deplores our inactivity.

"The tragedy is that it was necessary for her to come here to remind us of who we are, and to plead for our support for the heroic patriots. We are the ones upon whose shoulders rests the shame for having accepted with complacency the yoke of degradation which has befallen us. Shall we then act, not with determination, but with servitude, toward those who trample us with metal-shod boots into the hallowed ground saturated with the blood of our fathers?"

Murmurs of discomfort circled the chamber.

"The decision is ours," Hillel challenged. "The future of Judea lies in the hands of us who sit in judgment, who interpret the Law by which we live, and without whose support the defenders of Judea will have died in vain."

With a nod, Hillel let Shira know it was time for her to depart the chamber, leaving the elders to deliberate.

Now, she could only wait. From the Hall of Polished Stone, elbowing her way through the bustling masses, she felt a strong hand grab her wrist. Startled, she stared into the face of a Roman soldier. The crowd, sensing danger, fell away. Shira, with a determined twist of her arm, was able to free herself and run, in which direction she neither knew nor cared, her only thought to avoid arrest.

"After her!" an angry voice commanded.

CHAPTER 10

In his chambers of Herod's palace, Augustus Caesar, paced the floor, scarcely aware of the glistening inlaid gold of the tiles he trod. Oblivious, too, was he of the magnificent murals gracing the walls, luxurious Persian carpets, and embossed draperies covering the windows. His thoughts were of his empire, reflecting on the outcome of his session with Herod earlier in the day.

At age twenty, Augustus (then Octavian) had been ordained by his adoptive father, Julius Caesar, to succeed him as emperor of Rome. The youthful monarch accepted with grace the scepter of power, and ruled with tempered authority. His adoring subjects bestowed upon him the title of "Augustus," elevating him to the status of a god.

Under Augustus, the empire had thrived. The world he ruled was at peace, except for Judea, where the Jews continued to protest the tyrannical King Herod, the pawn of Rome, to which he was indebted for his kingship.

Augustus, an admirer of the tempestuous Herod, was convinced that the king was capable of appeasing, or coercing, the Judeans into submitting to Roman rule. After all, had the young Herod not put down insurrections in the Galilee? And had he not squelched fanatical uprisings against the empire in Judea? Even so, Augustus conceded, Herod's major successes were long ago. Was it possible that the king's aging mentality impaired his ability to rule? Crassus implied as much on the floor of the Senate. In his conversations with Herod, however, Caesar had discovered nothing that led him to respect less the man who occupied the throne of Judea. In their discussion, he recalled that the king's demeanor was humble and subservient. Caesar came away from his counsel with Herod, having discerned no evidence of excessive force among the people who tilled the soil. They harvested their crops, and paid taxes on plots of ground hardly larger than the coin which bore the emperor's likeness. Yet, Miletus had characterized Herod as a blood-thirsty tyrant who wrung from the desolate land his tribute to Rome.

Herod had assured his master that "the punishment is designed to fit the crime,"

and Caesar found no fault in him. Still he was disturbed by unrest among the Jews.

The emperor's reflections were interrupted by sounds of a commotion filtering through a window overlooking the palace grounds. Striding to the window, he drew aside the brocade drapery and was stunned by what he saw–a woman being beaten by two palace guards.

"What is the disturbance?" he asked a servant entering the chamber.

"Nothing serious, my lord," said the young man lightly. "Only the thrashing of some disobedient Jew."

Despite his tenuous sensitivity toward the Jews, Caesar bristled at the shallow dismissal of what appeared to be a flagrant incident.

"Only a thrashing?" he said.

"She's an outspoken Jewess who incites the locals

against Roman rule. When the guards moved to arrest her, she ran. Somehow she got past the gates and wound up in the palace grounds."

Caesar took another look out the window. The woman was lying prostrate on the pebbled courtyard, bleeding from the head. The guards, cursing angrily, kicking her unmoving body.

"A woman?" the emperor said. A Jewish woman is the cause of such a brutal incident? "Bring her to me!" he demanded.

"Yes, sire," said the young servant, quaking in his shoes, hastening his departure from the royal presence.

"And summon the officer of the guard immediately," Caesar called after him.

Moments later, before the emperor appeared the battered figure of Shira bas Haran, supported by two guards, each holding an arm. Her clothing was tattered, her face smeared with blood. Recognizing the officer of the guard as Major Cassio, she tried to break away.

Wherever evil raised its ugly head the haughty major seemed to appear.

Cassio gave her a shove toward Caesar who viewed her with a curious eye.

Quavering in the presence of a stern-faced man she didn't know, Shira wondered who he was, and why she had been brought before him. Judging by the splendor of the chamber, however, her muddled mind told her he must be important.

Because of the blood and the bruises, and the harsh treatment at the hands of the palace guards, almost Caesar's heart went out to her.

"What are the charges against this woman?" he demanded of Cassio.

"Inciting to riot, my lord," said Cassio, pleased to once again be serving the emperor.

Caesar showed no sign of recollection of his former

aide.

"You were inciting to riot?" Caesar said to Shira, thinking she did not appear capable of leading an uprising against the empire.

"Please, sir, I only–"

She was cut short by a cuff across the mouth by Cassio's hand. "You dare lie to Caesar?" he bellowed.

"Enough of that!" said the emperor.

Caesar! Shira trembled in fear."Hear my prayer, O Lord," she breathed. "Protect your own from the cruelty of the oppressor."

"By what name are you called?" Caesar said to her.

"My name, sir, is Shira bas Haran."

"And did you, Shira bas Haran, speak against the empire?"

Only briefly did she hesitate. With nothing more to lose, she saw no need to humble herself in the presence of the mighty. She squared her shoulders and, with the strongest voice she could muster, said, "I did, sir."

"And did you not know that such action is tantamount to treason, punishable by death?"

Awed as she was, still she was tempted to lash out at the ruler of the world, berating the mighty monarch, leveling a barrage of epithets at the tyrannical Herod, burying Rome in an avalanche of invective. Instead, she curbed her anger, and said simply, "Yes, sir, I did."

"Yet you disregarded the law. Did you not know what might happen to you for such actions?"

The law! she seethed in silence. She lowered her eyes, and said, "If it please the great Caesar, I cared more about what was happening to my people."

"Impudent fool!" Cassio snarled, raising his riding crop as if to strike her.

"Enough!" Caesar said, and Cassio lowered the whip."What is your name?" He said to Cassio.

"Why, I am Major Cassio, sire."

As if trying to recall something from the past, Caesar said, "Cassio?" The name meant nothing to him.

"Yes, sire." With a sharp salute, Cassio said, "I am honored to once again be of service to my lord."

"You are not beyond reproach in this matter," Caesar said. "Leave us."

Cassio, visibly shaken by Caesar's rebuke, grabbed Shira by an arm to escort her from the chamber.

"The woman will remain," said Caesar.

"As you wish, my lord," said Cassio, leading his men away.

Alone with the Roman emperor, Shira quaked in the presence of this man with the chiseled features, without whose approval the world would cease to turn. Seldom had she feared any man, but now she was struck by the reality that her fate was in the hands of this tall man with the short-cropped gray hair, the sharp nose, strong, jutting chin, and fierce dark eyes that pierced with dread the hearts of kings, setting him apart from all others. He was Caesar!

He tugged a length of broadcloth suspended from the ceiling,. Inviting Shira to sit on a satin-covered hassock, he seated himself on a sofa draped with purple velvet. A huge wooden door swung open, and through it glided a female Nabatean servant. In her shiny black splendor, she looked neither right nor left, proceeding directly to where the emperor waited. She bowed before him to receive his wishes.

Caesar ordered wine. "For my guest and me," he said. "And bring fresh water and a cloth to bathe her face."

The woman disappeared, returning shortly bearing a basin of water and a white towel with which she gently laved the blood from Shira's face. From a silver carafe she then poured wine into two silver goblets, and bowed her way out, having spoken not a word. At the door she paused briefly with a wan, woman-to-woman smile, as if empathizing with Shira's dilemma. Shira did not respond.

Not eager to savor wine in the presence of an adversary, Shira hesitated. In the company of the world's most powerful man, however, she yielded to the wisdom of doing as he did, sipping when he sipped

"Do I frighten you, Shira bas Haran?"said the monarch.

Recalling the horror of having her son dragged from her arms and bashed against the village wall, and how she had wished to rid the world of Romulo and the entire Roman empire, Shira now wished she could destroy this Caesar.

"Yes, sir," she said. "You do frighten me."

With a faint smile that disappeared as suddenly as it came, Caesar said, "I've heard that you Jews fear only your god. Yahweh, is it? Is it not strange, then, that you would be frightened of me?"

"It is no secret, sir, that all the world fears Caesar."

Her voice had not betrayed it, her attempt at humility did not reveal it, but rarely had Caesar seen such defiance as he saw smoldering in the eyes of his contentious guest.

"And though you fear me," said he, "you make little effort to conceal your hatred."

To mask her resentment in a facade of meekness would be futile. Caesar would tolerate nothing less than the truth. With all the courage of her Jewish heritage, therefore, she said, "Sir, may I speak frankly?"

"By all means," said Caesar with a curious smile. What could this peasant woman with the bruised face and tattered clothing say to him that he had not heard before."To seek truth," he said, "is to court wisdom."

Perhaps it was the wine that bolstered her courage. Or it could be that this was the moment for which she had been ordained–granting all mankind permission to speak with the tongue of Shira bas Haran. Whatever the source of her strength, Shira no longer trembled before the world's most powerful man.

Boldly she began to speak. "It is not against Caesar that the fires of Jewish resentment rage, sir, but against Rome, and against the infamy of the empire under whose boot we are ground into the earth."

"Boot?" said the monarch, his face reddening with the beginning of wrath. "The boot of Rome is the boot of Caesar. I am Rome!"

"Your pardon, sir, but did you not give me leave to speak frankly?"

"That I did, and frankly you shall continue to speak. Be aware, however, that when you condemn Rome, you condemn Caesar."

"Even so, sir, in Rome you are far removed from the suffering and the shame. Why you are here now I don't know, but I cannot believe that if the great Caesar were fully aware of the oppression against the people of Judea, he would tolerate the cruelty of the tyrannical Herod."

"I am aware," said Caesar curtly. With obvious restraint, again he said, "I am aware." Sipping the wine, he spent a moment recovering his composure. Why had he allowed this bedraggled peasant woman to upset him? Only to aid his appraisal of Herod's reign had he detained her, anticipating a conversation with one whose opinions and demeanor reflected the basic Jewish character.

His ignorance, however, denied him the knowledge that there was no such thing as the "basic Jewish character." Every Jew perceived himself as a wellspring of independent thought. What had begun as an accidental encounter with an obscure Jewess, therefore, had evolved into a political joust with a strong-willed young woman with a blood-smeared face and the audacity to speak her mind in the presence of the mighty.

"Then you must know, sir," said she, "that we are proud people, too proud to passively yield to such harsh treatment at the hands of Herod."

"I am aware that you endure stringent rules under King

Herod. You pay taxes that are galling to your proud people, and you are subjected to humiliating curfews and prohibitions of assembly. I know also that Herod has constructed new cities, amphitheaters, and water systems–and he has rebuilt your temple where you are free to worship. These are commendable achievements, characteristic of a king who cares about his people.

"I came here to meet with King Herod," Caesar said, "and I now believe that of all the leaders in the empire, he is most capable of maintaining the peace. Though he is indebted to Rome, I am convinced that he also is concerned for the welfare of your country." With an air of finality, he said, "You and your people must be content with the king's purposes and his methods. Herod is good for Judea."

It has been said that every Jew creates his own world, that he yields to no force, except his God, beyond that generated by himself, according to his individual determination, or influenced by his heritage. He may respond in agreement with other Jews, but only as an independent entity in union with other similarly inclined entities. He lit his own fires, and fought his own battles, and dealt with the consequences.

Driven by her Jewish birthright, Shira mounted her response to Caesar's support of the vassal king. From the depths of her persecuted, God-fearing ancestry, predating by thousands of years the birth of Rome, her venomous rejoinder burst forth.

"One day, O mighty Caesar," she hissed, releasing a flood of hostility that for countless generations had lain in wait for the appropriate time to explode in the face of the oppressor. "One day we will rise up against you and your murdering lackeys who suck the lifeblood from my people!"

"You speak treason!"

"With the strength of our God, we will destroy you–"

"Guard!"

"–and Rome will be remembered only for its cruelty, its greed, and its thirst for the blood of innocent people!"

"Guard!" the emperor shouted again.

Major Cassio rushed into the chamber, followed by the palace guards.

"My patience is at an end, Shira bas Haran," said Caesar, on the edge of rage. "Your audacity has carried you too far." To Cassio, he said, "Remove this woman!"

The guards laid hold of her.

Having tempted the fires of doom with nothing more to risk, Shira managed a defiant sneer, casting a final barb at the seething Caesar. "I suffer now," she shouted, as she was being dragged away, "not because of what I spoke, but because of the madness of Caesar, and the sins of his pagan murderers!"

"Away with her!" said Caesar. Only because he gave her leave to speak would she escape severe punishment, perhaps even death on the cross.

Clear of the emperor's quarters, Cassio snarled, "I should have had you flogged the first time I saw you!" He shoved her to the ground in the courtyard from which Caesar had rescued her a half hour before. Grabbing her by the shoulders, Cassio pulled her roughly to her feet, prodding her forward with his riding crop until she was clear of the palace gates. There she recognized Sergeant Quintas who was marching a column of captives to the prison camp near Beth-hoglah.

"Here's another one for you, sergeant," Cassio said. "She's the one you thought was a house maiden in the marketplace. Now she has insulted the emperor!"

"A saucy one, eh?" said Quintas. "They all look alike to me."

"You'll want to keep a close watch on this one."

"Aye, sir, that I will," Quintas said with an evil wink. "That I will." He grabbed at Shira, but she slapped his hairy hand away. The leering Quintas responded with a wicked laugh.

Falling in step with the column of prisoners, Shira looked neither right nor left. She remembered Quintas as the Roman who had beaten Rabbi Josef to death. Threatened more by Quintas than by Caesar, she feared what might happen to her before the march came to an end.

CHAPTER 11

In the lush green meadows near the Dead Sea, sheep grazed themselves slick, and crops, nourished by recent rainfall, flourished in the mild climate. West of the sea, desert hills lay barren, for seldom was there sufficient moisture to quench the thirst of the parched ravines. Summers without rain were hot and dry, plant growth ceased, and bare feet were blistered by the scorched earth. Now, the rainy season revived vegetation, providing ample nourishment for the flocks.

Through the jagged hills Judah ben Hezekiah mopped his sweat drenched brow, giving his roan stallion freedom to pick his way up a steep incline to where Shira had directed him in search of Romulo. Following single file was a troop of his heat-irritated comrades.

"Hold!"

Judah heard the sharp command, but saw no one. He halted his mount and raised his right hand, signaling his men to rein their mounts to.

From behind a boulder twenty paces ahead, Zacheas

appeared with his bow and arrow aimed at Judah's chest. Zacheas nodded his head, and within seconds Judah was surrounded by fierce-eyed rebels, bows at the ready, slings laden, long knives poised.

The Galileans moved to arm themselves, but Judah again raised a hand, signaling for calm.

"Who are you?" Zacheas demanded.

"My friends and I come from Galilee," said Judah.

Zacheas spat contemptuously.

"We come in peace," Judah said.

"Who are you?" Zacheas said again.

"I am Judah ben Hezekiah of Galilee, and these are my men." Again he said, "We come in peace."

"And I am Cleopatra," said Zacheas, prompting chuckles from his comrades.

An appreciative smile lit the face of Judah ben Hezekiah."Well said, my friend," said he. "With an army of men such as yourself the gorgeous lady might have taken the measure of Caesar, and be languishing yet in the arms of the lovesick Antony."

"Who are—"

"I am who I say I am," Judah said.

"Before I puncture your belly with an arrow," said Zacheas, "would the proud Galilean tell us why he has come to lowly Judea?"

"I come in search of your leader."

Zacheas shifted warily from one foot to the other."Romulo?" he said.

"Romulo de Vincius."

With threatening steps the rebels tightened the circle around Judah and his men.

"Hold, Zacheas!" came the command from behind the sentry, and all eyes turned as Romulo stepped forward. "You have done well, Zacheas," he said. "Judah ben Hezekiah is one of us. He is the leader of the Galilean patriots. Give way, and let him pass."

***

Far into the night, long after the fire reduced itself to a heap of gray ashes, Romulo and Judah talked. With mutual respect, they discussed the plight of their people. Debating, challenging each other's strategy for dealing with the Romans, they displayed similar strengths, and hopes for banishing the emperor worshipers from their lands.

"Does your coming to Judea," Romulo said, "mean that you have abandoned Galilee to Varus's vultures?"

"Abandoned? By no means. The conflict has been going on for much too long, and Galilee needs a rest. Withdrawing my troops leaves Varus no one to fight. Unlike Herod, he has no taste for killing helpless women and children. But he will still be there when we return. My men are dispersed in the hills," Judah went on, "many of them are already in Judea, and I am here to commit them, and myself, to your service."

"You and your men are much needed," said Romulo. "You know, of course, that Herod is after your head."

"He has never forgiven me for eluding his dragnet, and I have not forgiven him for murdering my father and my brothers."

Romulo clapped an appreciative hand on the shoulder of his guest.

"I have a message for you," Judah said, "from Shira bas Haran."

"She told you where to find me?"

"Yes, and something more. She loves you."

Romulo blinked. "She told you that?"

"She didn't have to. I saw it on her face when she spoke your name."

"Romulo!"

From outside the tent, the voice of Varisias penetrated the thin walls. Romulo stuck his head out the tent flap. "Over here," he said.

"They've got Shira."

CHAPTER 12

Romulo made no attempt to conceal his anger. Varisias and Judah, dispatched to Jerusalem to investigate, had returned with their report of the circumstances surrounding Shira's arrest.

"What are the charges?" Romulo said.

Varisias said, "Inciting to riot, resisting arrest, and–" He took a deep breath. "–threatening the emperor."

"Caesar?" Romulo was aghast. "Shira threatened Caesar?"

"Those are the charges," Judah said. "Shira met with the Council and was leaving the Hall of Polished Stones when she was recognized by a guard. When the guard tried to arrest her for anti-Roman remarks in the market place, she ran."

Finally, Romulo thought, Shira had been called to appear before the Council. There was no time now to consider the result of her appearance. "How did it happen?" he said to Judah.

Having observed a similar incident in the market place,

Judah knew well the kinds of remarks Shira must have made."Somehow she got away," he said, ending his account of the circumstances, "and wound up in the palace grounds."

Varisias said, "Caesar rescued her from a beating by the palace guards. Your old friend Cassio was the officer of the guard."

"Caesar rescued her?" Romulo said, heading for the door. "There is no time to lose. Where are they holding her?"

"In that old prison camp outside Beth-hoglah," Varisias said.

"I know that camp," Romulo said. "Varisias, alert the men. Thirty should be enough. The Romans have never had much of a force there to guard the prisoners. And, Varisias, you'll come with me. You know that country as well as I do. If we get separated, the mission can still be carried out," To Judah, he said, "Can I count on you to be in command here while we're gone?"

"You can."

***

Shira was herded, along with the column of prisoners, into a stockade carved out of the hills. There were women and children who didn't know why they were there, though most of the prisoners were men with crude, loosely wrapped bandages around their heads, arms and legs. All showed signs of fear, fully aware that they could be living their last days.

Shira went about doing what she could to comfort those who couldn't care for themselves, adjusting bandages, helping the lame to walk, dispensing food and water, of which there was little. Incensed by the Roman guards who stuffed themselves with food in the presence of the hungry children, she could no longer abide their arrogance. With a final defiant twist she patted a bloody bandage covering the leg of an elderly man who was beaten for not giving way to a Roman officer in the marketplace. Wiping her hands on the front of her soiled robe, she threw back her head, squared her shoulders, and marched off with determined strides straight for the quarters of the camp commander. At the door of his tent she demanded that the youthful orderly permit her to see the commander, Colonel Marius.

The orderly, ogling her with lustful eyes, touched her face with a sweaty hand.

Shira slapped his hand away. "Stand aside," she said, "or I'll scratch your bloody eyes out!"

"Why, you little wench," the orderly said, raising a hand to strike her."I'll show you."

In a fury, Shira bared her nails, curled her fingers in a catlike motion, and went for his face.

The orderly threw up his arms to fend off her charge. Backing away from the threat of a scarred face, he pulled aside the flap of the commander's tent. "By your leave, sir," he said, "a caller." He moved aside, with a close eye on Shira as she stepped into the tent.

Round-shouldered and bug-eyed, the rotund Colonel Marius sat slumped over a small table covered with documents. His bald head was suspended above the table like a gray-fringed melon. Peering up through weary eyes, Marius was astonished to see fuming in his doorway a handsome young woman. Even with her smudged face and tattered clothing she was a striking temptation for the puffy-faced colonel. Regarding with eagerness the flashing brown eyes and sensuous lips, the fire of a rare emotion seared his loins.

"I am Shira bas Haran," she announced in a strong voice. "I have come to protest the abominable treatment of the women and children in this camp."

"The women and children," the colonel said, his mind

elsewhere.

"The accommodations are totally inadequate, the children suffer from too little food, and your soldiers indulge their gluttonous appetites in their presence, causing the children even greater discomfort."

Colonel Marius appraised her with an inquisitive eye. His dealings were with men who humbled themselves before him, seeking his favor. Now, here stood this woman, neither humble nor respectful of his authority, displaying brazen aggressiveness. Briefly he wished for a legion of soldiers with as much courage, motioning her to a wooden stool in the middle of the tent.

"Won't you sit down, Miss–"

"Shira bas Haran."

"Yes."

"I'll stand if–"

"Please," he said firmly, asserting his authority. "Sit down."

She sat.

"I dislike having to look up to people when I talk to them," Marius said, making no effort to stand. "Now, I believe you said something about the treatment of the women and children. And you are one of them?"

"I am."

"And what were the charges against you?"

"Nobody told me."

"What were the circumstances surrounding your arrest?"

Shira hesitated. Should she tell him she berated the emperor? She suspected the colonel already knew the answers to his questions, since a report doubtless accompanied her arrival there.

"I was having a–conversation–with the emperor," she said.

A faint smile touched the colonel's thick lips. Here then, standing unabashedly before him, pleading for the welfare of her fellow prisoners, was the peasant woman who verbally attacked Caesar, disparaging him and the Roman empire. Marius marveled that she had not been stoned, or even crucified with her naked body nailed to a cross with her head down.

"And now," he said with mounting admiration for her spirit, "you have taken it upon yourself to champion the cause of the women and children in my camp."

"They're so frightened they can't speak for themselves, and they don't even know why they're here."

"They are here, Shira bas Haran, because their husbands and fathers engaged in warfare against the empire."

"Are the children, then, accountable for the actions of their fathers?"

The colonel rose, facing her with a wan smile. As he talked, the smile faded. "The business of war is a hellish endeavor," said he. "It is not always justified, and it is rarely fair. The guilty are not always punished, and the innocent are not always vindicated. Whatever the circumstances, however, it is imperative that Rome utilize all available means to avert defeat."

Shira got to her feet, facing him with a defiant wave. "And these women and children," she said. "Are they considered enemies of the empire?"

Marius took a moment to formulate a response. Why was he sparring with this peasant woman? What right had she to question the motives of the Roman empire? He was beginning to understand the circumstances of her encounter with the emperor. Yet, in the hungry eyes of Colonel Marius, she was a more sophisticated young woman than he would have expected of one of her humble heritage. She had fire in her eyes and spirit in her soul, a woman who could make a man feel whole again.

"Anyone who is not fighting for us is fighting against us," he said. "Rome's purposes are not always noble, but they are never foolhardy."

"What has that to do, sir, with no food for hungry children, and no medication for the wounded?"

Flipping through a file, the colonel brought out a document and began reciting the charges against her. "Shira bas Haran: Sedition, inciting to riot, attacking the emperor, and treason—punishable by death." He replaced the file and faced her with a blank expression. "And Sergeant Quintas tells me that you also resisted arrest. Is that true?"

"Is it truth you want, colonel, or confirmation of the charges against me?"

"Are you aware," he said, "that because of these charges I could have you put to death, and it would be carried out immediately?" He did not wait for an answer. Instead, he rose and took a step toward her, so close that she could feel the heat of his heaving body. "We are all possessed of animal instincts, Shira bas Haran," said he through quivering lips, devouring her with his large round eyes. "I'm a reasonable man, and I'm the only one who can help you make life more bearable for the women and children." She felt his hot breath on her face. "Perhaps there is something you can do for me."

She did not need a prophet to interpret the colonel's bold proposal.

"I know how concerned you are for your fellow prisoners," he said. "And I admire your courage in coming here."

Seething inside, Shira tried to move away, but he grabbed her with beefy arms and crushed her to his flabby body, kissing her roughly on the mouth. He buried his sweating face in the white softness of her throat, fumbling at her clothing with clammy hands.

Struggling to free herself, Shira's hand stroked the dagger strapped to his side. Instinctively she closed her fingers around the hilt, yanking it from its scabbard. Into the back of the unsuspecting Roman she plunged the blade, stabbing and twisting until his head lolled crazily, his eyes reflecting shock and disbelief. With a furious gasp, Marius released her, and crumpled in a lifeless heap at her feet.

Transfixed by his staring, unseeing eyes, Shira's fingers froze around the bloody dagger. Never before had she held a weapon. Loathing it as an instrument of evil, she briefly considered tossing it aside. Then, in her precarious predicament, she thought she might need the sword to defend herself should she be discovered.

Beyond the tent walls the sounds of anxious voices alerted her to the danger of being found in the quarters of the camp commander, clutching the dagger dripping with the blood of the boorish Roman. The commotion outside aroused in her the fear that her deed would soon be known, prompting her to grasp more securely the hilt of the short sword.

From somewhere she heard the ear-shattering blare of a ram's horn. The rebels' battle call! The sound of hope that she could safely escape. Did they know she was in the prison? If so, would they arrive in time to save her from certain death if the guards found her?

Through the walls of the tent burst the sound of running, heavy-booted feet, Roman officers shouting orders.

The young orderly stuck his head in the door of the colonel's tent, and yelled, "Colonel, sir, the rebels are approaching from the– "

The blade of the colonel's dagger in the hand of Shira bas Haran split the orderly's belly. His voice went silent, his face contorted in shock. His body plopped to the floor, spurting blood that mingled with that of the colonel, forming red craters in the dusty tent floor.

Shira held the sword in her right hand. With her left she cautiously drew aside the tent flap. Frenzied camp guards, alerted by the chilling sound of the ram's horn, dashed about, some on foot, others on horseback. An officer screamed orders in a feverish effort to mount a defense against the onrushing rebels.

The prisoners, confused and frightened by the flurry of activity, huddled together, mothers hugging their frightened children to their breasts.

The blood-curdling cries of the patriots grew louder as they stormed closer to the prison camp.

Shira seized the opportunity to escape the colonel's tent. Skirting the mass of frenetic activity, she sprinted toward the gate through which she knew the rebels would storm the compound.

She never reached the gate. A Roman on a white horse dashed by, grabbed her by an arm, and wrested the knife out of her hand.

"You filthy swine!" she hissed, recognizing him as the leering Sergeant Quintas.

He lifted her by the shoulders, forcing her to lie face down in front of him across the horse's neck. She kicked and screamed, struggling to free herself, but she could not break the grasp of the Roman's burly arms.

He spurred the stallion into a dead run, cleared the compound, and headed south.

The rebels swarmed through the north gate of the rock-bound enclosure, slashing and jabbing at the outnumbered guards. Within minutes the Roman contingent was crushed.

Romulo reined his mount to a halt."Hold there, Varisias!" he shouted, dismounting.

The centurion stepped up beside him."One thing I've learned," said Varisias, "is that Romans bleed the same as everybody else."

Moving toward a group of sallow-faced children whose mothers hovered about them, to Varisias, Romulo said, "Take a couple of men and round up what food you can find and lay it out for them–the women and children first."

Quick-stepping away, Varisias called, "Simon, Zebulon, over here on the double!"

Romulo headed to the commander's tent, dagger drawn. Anticipating a challenge, he yanked aside the flap of Marius's tent, and was shocked to find the bodies of the colonel and his orderly sprawled on the floor in pools of blood.

From behind him he heard the voice of a woman, short, gray-haired with deep creases in her leathery brown face. "There was a young woman," she said to Romulo. "She was kind to us, and she was not afraid of the Romans."

"A young woman? Do you know her name?"

"I heard it once but– Maybe Sara? Sira?"

"Shira?"

"I think so, yes. Shira."

"When did you last see her?"

"A short while ago, just before you came. I saw her come to this tent, but I never saw her again."

Romulo glanced at the bodies and wondered whether Shira was the last person to see the colonel and the orderly alive. Where was she now?

"I saw her," said a slender girl of twelve beside the woman. "She went into the tent, then when all the noise started she came running out. A Roman soldier on a white horse grabbed her and carried her away. He rode off that way," said the girl, pointing to the south. "I heard someone call him Quintas. He was mean to us."

"Thank you. You have done well." Turning away, he called, "Varisias!"

Varisias handed his food basket to Zebulon and met Romulo in the middle of the compound. "Have you found Shira?" Varisias said.

Striding briskly toward his horse, Romulo said, "No, but these people say they saw a Roman carry her away on a white horse. I'm going after her." He swung into the saddle.

"See to the women and children, then get word to Judah to delay any further action until I return unless he is attacked."

"Yes, sir. Will you ride alone?"

"I will ride alone." He spurred the gray forward. "There's only one Roman on a white horse. There can't be many of those between here and Beth-hoglah. He's probably headed for the outpost there."

"Romulo!" Varisias called to his back. "Walk close to the wall!"

Romulo nodded, urging the stallion into the hills heading south.

***

Quintas jerked the horse up short; looking around to be sure no one was coming up behind him. "Nobody yet," he said as if to himself.

Shiny with sweat, the skittish horse frothed at the mouth, nostrils flared. With one hand Quintas struggled to calm him, while keeping his squirming captive under control with the other.

"They will be coming!" Shira said. "And when they do—"

"And when they do, my pretty little piece," Quintas said with a licentious laugh, "you will be my safe passage to wherever I want to go. Make no mistake about that. I know who you are, and Major Cassio would give a fortune to get you in his clutches."

Shira fought to free herself.

"Here now!" said Quintas, as if to a playful child. "No need for that. The time will come when you'll be glad to feel old Quintas's lovin' arms around you." He roared a wicked laugh and buried a heel in the horse's flank.

***

Romulo followed the ages old trail across the desert. Beth-hoglah was the site of the nearest Roman outpost, and he was certain that was where he would find Quintas. He dared not think beyond that, though doubting not that the Roman would take Shira for himself if he wanted, then slit her throat and dump her ravaged body along the desert trail.

He spurred the gray into a full gallop.

***

At the Inn of the Red Fox in Beth-hoglah, half a dozen young wine-soaked legionaries sat around a table, trading stories about escapades of the night before, boasting with loud voices of their amorous conquests. The more they drank, the louder they laughed, shouting at each other the bawdy details.

"More wine!" one of them demanded, and Trobah, the fat-faced innkeeper, appeared with a fresh pitcher.

"I guess you saw Sergeant Quintas ride in," said another, carelessly tipping his wine bowl until it spilled down the front of his uniform.

"I saw him," said his neighbor. "He looked haggard as a ghost. Like he had just spent a week in bed with one of your whores."

That elicited a round of derisive laughter.

"That was no ghost Quintas brought with him," said another.

"You mean that dark-haired little piece with the snarl of a wolf? I wonder where he found her."

"There was some talk about a fracas at the prison camp up north."

"If she's a prisoner," said a mild mannered recruit, "wouldn't Quintas have to turn her over to the authorities?"

Suffering a round of derisive guffaws, the recruit's face

turned an embarrassing red.

"You mean after he has had his fill of her?" his neighbor scoffed.

"Regulations require that all prisoners be reported within–" The recruit was cut short by another round of laughter.

"Regulations be damned! She's not a prisoner of war. She's a captive of Sergeant Quintas!"

"When he's through with her, he'll chew her up and spit her out."

"More wine!"

***

For seven years Quintas had hoped for a promotion in rank, but every year he had been passed over in favor of some politically connected oaf with no military experience. Now, however, he could not believe his good fortune. Now, he assured himself, his time had come, for he held in his grasp a hostage, giving him some bargaining power.

He checked his grip on his captive to be sure it was secure.

Quintas had not planned to kidnap Shira nor anyone else until the moment it happened. Blaring of the ram's horn, signaling the rebels attack on the prison compound, alerted him to the need to be gone.

Taking someone with him had not been a part of his plan when he leaped into the saddle of the first horse he saw. Driven by animal instinct for self preservation, he grabbed Shira on the way out. Not until later did he recognize her as the woman Cassio shoved into Quintas's column of prisoners. "She insulted the emperor," Cassio had told him.

Quintas's future grew bright with promise as he became aware of the catch he had made, assuring for him a life of luxury. Cassio would pay a handsome price for this luscious little vixen. If she earned him no promotion, the least Quintas could hope for was a healthy ransom for her release. Already he pictured himself languishing in the luxury of a huge estate with dozens of obedient slaves, and gorgeous women falling over themselves to do his bidding. In his satanic fantasy, Quintas stood to reap a rich harvest from his capture of the brazen little trouble maker held flat on her belly across his saddle.. Even so, he would not release her until he had squeezed from this delicious bit of fruit the last drop of succulent nectar.

***

At the Inn of the Red Fox, Romulo was greeted by its lumpy proprietor, Trobah. Fat and beady-eyed, Trobah smelled of sweat and sour wine. An ingratiating smile split his heavy black beard. "Ah, my friend," said he with a familiar air, placing a bowl of wine on the table in front of Romulo. "A man of the road, I see. You doubtless will want a large tub of hot water to wash away the dust, and wine that cures all ills."

"Perhaps," said Romulo. "But first I want some information. A man of your position sees and hears much."

Trobah viewed him with a wary eye."What is it that you want to know?" he said.

"A man named Quintas rode this way."

Romulo's eyes followed those of the innkeeper as they strayed to the table where sat the reveling young Roman soldiers. Trobah's thought likely was to expose Romulo to the legionaries, but he did not. Perhaps in the pockets of this stranger jingled a handful of coins which he might be willing to pay for the information he sought.

"I do not deal in information," Trobah said.

"Quintas was last seen in the company of a young woman–a Jewess. I'm told that you know all that goes on around here," Romulo said. "If it's money you want, I'm willing to pay." Romulo dropped a few coins on the table.

At sight of the coins the innkeeper eyes grew big. " On the other hand–" he said.

With the sleeve of his robe he wiped his sweating brow. "If I tell you, he will kill me," he said. "And if I don't tell you–"

Romulo watched the sweat beads trickle down the flabby cheeks of the greedy Trobah. A deep sigh escaped the innkeeper's puffy lips as he spread his arms in a gesture of hopelessness. Money was money from whatever source, and what he saw on the table would compensate for betrayal.

"At the Inn of the Seven Moons," he said. "But he has hard-nosed friends who–"

"Don't try to deceive me, innkeeper," Romulo said.

"What I tell you is the truth. I'm told that Quintas arrived within the hour at the Inn of the Seven Moons."

"And the woman?"

"Yes, the woman also."

Romulo turned on a heel."If it is not as you say, I'll be back."

Trobah raked the coins into his palm, and peered across the room. Near the exit stood a man with his eyes locked on Trobah's as if awaiting instructions. Trobah gave him a furtive nod. The man at the door slipped out into the night.

***

Shira cringed as the fumbling Quintas fondled a strand of her hair. Major Cassio had done the same, and it was no less disgusting now than then.

"You've no cause to be afraid of old Quintas, missy," Quintas said with a wicked laugh that made the knife scar on his right cheek even uglier. He seldom smiled, but often laughed. "I need you to get me that promotion I've waited for. I hadn't served enough time, the captain said. Only six years. I needed more seasoning, he said. Oh, that captain," he said with a malicious laugh. "Captain Romulo de Vincius."

Shira's ears perked up.

"He was tough, but he was fair." Quintas went on. "It wasn't his fault. He had to answer to the biggies above him. He had a soft spot though, Romulo did. When Herod issued his decree– Remember the decree, missy?"

A wave of revulsion swept through Shira's body that this animal should even mention Herod's slaughter of the innocents.

"I hear the captain is leading a band of rebel raiders now," Quintas said. "When he gets caught, all he's got to look forward to is a spear in the belly. Or maybe spread-eagled on a cross." From a pedestal he grabbed a wineskin and gulped a mouthful, dribbling it over his chin."You know, missy, I've got myself a real problem. I can't make up my mind what to do with you. I could turn you over to the post outside of town, but if I did that, those young jacks who saw me bring you in would try to take you away from me." He grabbed her chin in his left hand. "You wouldn't want that to happen, would you, missy? You wouldn't want old Quintas to lose his promotion just so a few young jacks could frolic about some, now would you?"

She slapped his hand away and spat in his face.

Quintas struck her across the mouth with a back-hand that knocked her against the wall. He flung her onto the bed, stifling her cries with a calloused hand over her mouth.

Shira fought to free herself from the raging Roman, but was no match for his brute strength. He stripped away her robe, and mauled her tender thighs, leaving ugly red marks on her delicate skin. With groping hands he massaged her naked breasts until they bled, laughing the while with a guttural sound that drenched her body with torrents of loathing.

The harder she fought, the louder he laughed, like a scavenging hyena.

***

Along the narrow winding street Romulo melted into the bustling throng of traders, peasants, hawkers of wares, and Roman soldiers who paid him no mind. Beth-hoglah was one of many villages where brigands, footpads, and ruffians sought refuge, any one of whom would have slashed a man's throat for a coin. Varisias had cautioned Romulo to "walk close to the wall." Romulo did so with a wary eye, pushing his way toward the Inn of the Seven Moons.

Turning toward the inn, his path was blocked by a brawny man with massive arms spread like a wounded bear. Romulo ducked away, but a second assailant leaped on him from behind, screaming curses, nudging his throat with the point of a blade. Romulo seized the back of the man's head and hurled him onto the rocky pathway. The attacker limped away with cries of pain.

The first man swung at him with a two-edged knife. Romulo sidestepped the blow and drew his short sword. The ruffian swung again, but missed, and Romulo stepped inside

his flailing arms and buried his dagger in the attacker's chest. The man keeled over, blood pouring from the wound, shivered convulsively, then breathed no more.

Romulo glanced about for an accomplice who might assume the attack. Seeing no one, he sheathed his weapon and moved on to the Inn of the Seven Moons.

"A Roman named Quintas," he said to a slight young man carrying a bowl of wine in each hand.

"Quintas?" said he, eager to be gone.

Romulo held out a coin, and the young man took an anxious look around.

"I was told he was here at the Inn of the Seven Moons," Romulo said, flashing a coin.

"Upstairs at the end of the hall," said the server. He bared his teeth and Romulo placed the coin between them.

"The woman?" Romulo said.

The server nodded and hurried away.

Romulo found the stairway, mounting the steps two at a time. Reaching the landing, he heard the muffled cries of a woman in a nearby room. Cautiously, he slipped into the room. Shira was struggling under the bulk of the boorish Quintas.

Romulo pounced on the Roman and grabbed him by the throat.

Quintas felt the pressure of strong hands closing with a vise like grip. His mouth flew open, his eyes growing big, unbelieving. Romulo smashed Quintas's head against the wall.

Shira wriggled free, snatched up her robe. She drew it around her naked body, and hovered in a corner.

Jabbing and punching, Romulo was on top of the bewildered Roman. Quintas wrestled free, and scrambled to his feet. He swung in a wide arc that missed, and Romulo floored him with a blow to the head. The snarling Quintas regained his footing, and whipped out his sword. Quick as a heartbeat his challenge was answered when Romulo flashed his dagger.

"Aha!" said the Roman with a vicious laugh. "We meet again, Captain Romulo!"

"Again?"

"So! Not only do I not get a promotion," Quintas sneered with a wild stab, "but I am not even remembered for my service!"

Romulo's slash to the arm of the incensed Roman brought blood. At sight of his bleeding arm, Quintas raised his dagger above his head, growled fiercely, and threw his weight into a hacking blow. Romulo eluded the effort.

Quintas lunged at him, catching Romulo's chin with one hand, pressing the point of his dagger to his throat with the other. Romulo locked both hands around Quintas's knife hand, struggling to avoid the blade. Reaching deep for all his strength he twisted the knife from the Roman's grasp, and heard it drop to the floor.

Quintas made a dive for the sword, but Romulo scrambled to his feet and floored him with a double-fisted blow to the head.

Romulo grabbed the dagger, and turned the point toward the ceiling. In a frantic leap to recover the weapon, Quintas fell on the upturned blade and stabbed himself in the chest. His hand went to the blood-spurting wound in open-mouthed disbelief, wild-eyed, peering at his bloody fingers. With a look at Shira, as if pleading for mercy, he groaned once, rolled onto his side, exhaled heavily, and died.

"We must hurry," Romulo said to Shira, "before someone discovers the body. I'll see you to safety."

"No," Shira said. "I'll be all right."

"How will you get back to Bethlehem? You must let me help you. I can't leave you here."

"Alone you can travel faster."

"Shira–"

"Romulo–"

"Yes?"

She sought words to tell him what she wanted him to know, what she felt for him, but no words came. "I'll manage," she said . "You're the one they want."

"No matter. Already my life is worth nothing if they find me."

She took a deep breath."I too have killed," she said. Romulo was not surprised to hear her say, "At the prison camp–with the colonel's dagger."

"It was you then," he said, admiring her courage.

"They were mistreating the women and children. I

went to protest, and the camp commander attacked me."

"Shira."

"Please, Romulo, you must hurry."

He nodded toward Quintas's body. "If they find you here—"

"Better me than you. Judea needs you."

"And you!"

"Please go, Romulo. You're wasting precious time."

His senses cried out to sweep her up and carry her to safety, even as her pleading eyes screamed the folly of his doing so. With a reluctant goodbye, his eyes sought hers, then he was gone.

CHAPTER 13

Shira slipped out of the room and down the back stairs to the trade center where she would seek passage to Bethlehem. At the staging area she was greeted by a graying middle-aged man with a warm but authoritative voice.

"Might you be going to Jerusalem, miss?" he said.

"Jerusalem?" Yes, she said, though Bethlehem would be her destination. Once she got to Jerusalem, it would be a short journey home. "Yes," she said. "I am going to Jerusalem."

"I am Belthad, a wine trader on my way to the market in Jerusalem. If you care to do so, you're welcome to join my party, and we'll see you safely there."

"I have no money," she said. "I can't pay you for your kindness."

"There's no need for that. Your passage has been arranged."

"Arranged? By whom?"

"A friend of mine," with a tug at an ear lobe. "And

yours. A man named Romulo."

"Oh," she said with a grateful smile.

Belthad escorted her to a two-wheeled oxcart, and helped her onto a seat beside a young man holding the reins.

To Belthad, she said, "My name is–"

"Please," he said quickly, "do not tell me your name." His eyes darted about to see who might be within earshot. "We must be cautious. It is best that I not know who you are."

"Then how–"

"Romulo asked me to see you safely to Jerusalem. That I agreed to do. Beyond that I need know nothing."

With a terse nod, Belthad was off, shouting orders to drivers and animal handlers as he went. No further word would pass between himself and Shira.

In the caravan were seven oxcarts and an assortment of braying donkeys, along with half a dozen squawking camels laden with jewelry, tapestry, fine linens, carpets, and wines from distant lands. Bound for the lucrative market in Jerusalem, several traders had banded together to strengthen their defense against possible attacks by brigands along the way.

Shira heard Belthad shout an order, and the caravan began creaking forward. Donkeys and camels swayed rhythmically under the weight of bundles strapped to their sides. Oxen strained into hand-carved wooden yokes, plodding along the rocky trail, pulling carts piled high with merchandise.

Belthad chose to travel at night to escape the blistering daytime heat. Already, as he gave the order for the caravan to move out, the sun dipped behind the low-lying western hills.

"Do you want to make talk?" said the young man on the seat beside Shira.

She was startled by the sound of his voice, for until

now he had said nothing. "What?" she said.

"Make talk," he said. "Do you want to make talk?"

The boy was about sixteen, slender, dark haired, his face almost black from exposure to the sun. She shook her head no.

"He is a good man," said he.

Her thoughts were of Romulo, and whether he had escaped safely from Beth-hoglah.

The lad noticed her questioning look. "My master, Belthad," he said. "He is a good man. But there are some who are not so good."

Shira made no reply, her eyes on the oxens' swaying rumps, swishing their tails at her feet.

"My name is Shukar," the lad volunteered. "My friends call me Shukie. Some people call me a chatterbox because I talk most all the time. My father used to say that one who does not talk shares no wisdom with his friends." He cast Shira a quizzical look."You don't talk much," he said. "Does that mean that you have no wisdom to share with your friends?"

So outgoing was Shukar that Shira felt ashamed for her lack of enthusiasm for conversation.

"You may call me Shukie if you like," the boy went on.

"Thank you. I will call you Shukie."

He smiled, and flicked the reins along the backs of the stolid oxen.

"Where is your father now?" Shira said.

"My father is dead. He was killed when he and some friends attacked a Roman supply train. But," he said, "they will not attack this one. My master supports the rebels, and, since the Council refused to help them–"

Shira had not heard of the Council's decision. "Are you sure, Shukie–about the Council?"

"A friend of Belthad's sent word this morning. But Belthad will help them. He brings them food and clothing, and medicine when he can find it. He is a good man, my master."

With a heavy heart, Shira settled into silence. Hillel had spoken so poignantly in support of the rebels–but even he had not been able to sway the Council in their favor of the patriots. Sunset in Judea brought plunging temperatures, often below freezing. From under the cart seat, Shukar brought a woolen shawl and spread it across Shira's lap. She thanked him, drawing it about her shoulders against the chill of waning daylight.

Contemplating the Council's disappointing decision, her heart rode with Romulo–to safety? Or to danger?

Over the craggy, waterless hills the caravan ground its laborious way toward the safety of Jerusalem. Alive with the sounds of chattering birds, and the howl of a distant wolf, the night was clear and cold, bathed in the glow of a flawless moon and yellow, winking stars that seemed close enough to touch.

Shira's sleep was measured in catnaps, waking often by the roughness of the jostling oxcart. Through the night she heard the voice of Belthad, sometimes harsh, but always encouraging the men and animals, pushing the caravan forward. He dared not stop along the way for fear of attack by roving highwaymen. Shira wondered when he slept.

Shukar stirred beside her. "You are not sleeping, miss?" he said.

She shook her head.

"Some say the oxen don't sleep," he said. "But they don't know if I sleep, so they keep going until they feel the tug to stop, then they know I am not sleeping. The ox moves at one pace only, and it is said that he lives his whole life waiting for the tug, for he doesn't like to work. While he is waiting, I sleep a bit."

In the mystical time when day began to separate itself from night, the caravan trudged down from the ridges east of the Mount of Olives. Only the creaking oxcarts, and squawks of temperamental camels, disturbed the silent birth of a new day.

The caravan came to a sudden halt.

Shira cast Shukar a questioning glance. He was already on his feet. Peering into

the gray dawn, he saw Belthad at the head of the caravan, with his right hand held high, signaling the caravan to halt. From the east came the rumble of thundering hoof beats.

"Romans!" Shukie spat.

"Romans?" said Shira "What could they–"

"Shh!" he cautioned. "Do not talk now."

She heard voices laced with tension, but could not distinguish the exchange of words between Belthad and the Romans.

"One of them is dismounting," Shukar whispered. "The Roman is angry! He's pushing Belthad aside. The Roman is coming this way!"

Belthad followed closely behind the Roman officer who was examining each cart and wagon as he passed, lifting the cargo covers, scanning the faces of the travelers. He worked his way along the column until he reached Shukar's cart.

Shira froze. Had they found the body of the ignominious Quintas? What if they had already taken Romulo?

The Roman lifted the tarp covering Shukar's cart and peered underneath. A moment passed as he replaced the cover, and turned away. Pausing then, he looked back at the terrified Shira, flipping aside the mantle hiding her face.

Shira caught a quick breath, her tongue paralyzed, her heart racing so she feared the Roman might hear it pound. Did he know about Quintas? Was he searching for her? What about Romulo?

The hint of a smile touched the thin lips of the

inquisitive Roman."You are not Romulo," said he. With a gentle tug he replaced her mantle, turned on a heel, and was gone.

Not until she heard the rhythmic barrage of departing hoof beats did Shira allow herself to draw an easy breath. Romulo had escaped. But for how long?

***

The light of day faded into dusk as Romulo reached the valley's treeless floor, framed by walls of limestone and red dirt as far as he could see. Along the west wall, misty blue shadows clung like smoke to the base of the mountain.

Hugging the wall, he sought to shield himself from bands of marauders roaming the hills, preying on unwary travelers. Once the sun disappeared, taking with it its blast of merciless heat, a biting chill would take its place. Already Romulo could see his breath forming puffy white clouds.

Eyes alert to any sign of danger, he gave the gray his head, allowing him to pick his way across gullies and blistering limestone not yet cooled by the lengthening shadows. Once, the stallion skittered aside to escape an avalanche of boulders tumbling to the valley floor. On they pressed, horse and rider, through the shapeless hills, scarred by untold centuries of harsh winds, rain, and brutal heat.

Chilled by the swirling desert winds of night, even so, Romulo dared not make camp, for setting a fire would attract the bandits whose refuge was the rugged Judean hills.

Indeed, hardly had he entered the valley before he was struck by the unmistakable rumble of hoof beats. He buried a heel in the flank of the gray as man and animal became one, flying through the night, racing over bald hills and jagged gorges with the brigands in pursuit. The outlaws knew the wilderness as well as Romulo, urging him to push the gray even harder to reach the safety of the lowlands ahead, where a lone rider could easily outdistance a band of a dozen or more.

Not until he reached the banks of the Jordan did Romulo pause, listening for sounds of the pursuing raiders. What he heard was the calming trill of a single night bird, and the occasional growl of a restless leopard prowling the river banks in darkness as silent as the world it covered.

Reining the gray toward the rebel camp, he savored already the cup of hot broth Zacheas would have waiting. Unprepared was he, however, for the shocking news that awaited him there.

From the sands of Moab the rising sun splashed across the Jordan River, flooding

Judea with the promise of a new day. The mournful cry of a hungry dog in search of breakfast echoed across the thirsty hills as Romulo nudged the gray up a rocky slope to the rebel camp.

All night he had ridden, thinking of little except concern for Shira's safety. Had she made contact with Belthad? If so, he knew his friend would see her safely to Jerusalem. If not, what had become of her?

Greeted in the compound by the gentle nickering of restless horses, his nostrils were attacked by the musty odor of campfires stoked and rekindled to keep them alive through the night.

With a sharp salute, a sentry waved him into camp.

"Romulo," said Judah, falling in step beside him."Herod is dead."

CHAPTER 14

News of Herod's death swept the land of Judea like wheat from a broken bag. Hardly had the sounds of hoof beats and clanking armor of Caesar's entourage leaving for Alexandria died away before shouts of joy filled the air. Herod was dead!

It was common knowledge that for several years the king had suffered a life threatening disease. In the hot baths along the Jordan River he had found no relief from the malady tormenting his dissipated body.

Stunned by reports of the king's demise, still the wary Jews were skeptical of the truth of reports that the blood-thirsty despot had died. Until some trustworthy soul had viewed the lifeless body, they dared not believe. Rampant had been the fear that Herod would never die, and that they would forever be trapped in the web of his tyranny.

Herod's fruitless quest for a cure had left him nowhere to turn, except to a sick bed in his palace at Jerusalem. On his return from the banks of the Jordan, he was infuriated by reports that two rabbis and forty of their young disciples had torn from the gate of the temple the huge, glaring golden eagle installed as a tribute to his Roman benefactors. Any such display defied Jewish law prohibiting such images, and the rabbis' young charges had slid down ropes and smashed with axes the blasphemous golden eagle.

The incensed king miraculously revived long enough to stagger forth and berate the multitude of Judeans who witnessed the spectacle.

"You dare insult Caesar?" Herod bellowed, chafing yet from the Jews' insulting reception of his idolized emperor. "When you insult Caesar, you put to shame your beloved king, Herod the Great. And Herod shall not be shamed!"

At his command, the guards swarmed into the crowd, slashing with swords and knives. When the slaughter was over, three thousand Judeans lay dead. The forty students and their mentors the king condemned to death by burning them alive.

Having avenged the Judeans' affront to Caesar, Herod was bodily removed, coughing and wheezing, to his palace in Jericho to be near the hot springs where once again he sought relief from the intestinal affliction that was eating him alive. Five days later he was dead, but not before he ordered, with his final death bed gasp, the death of his eldest son Antipater whom Herod accused of conspiring against him.

The gigantic, bowl-shaped Herodium carved out of the earth, long ago had been decreed as Herod's final resting place. The nine-mile processional route from his Jericho palace to the tomb was lined with thousands of Jews. They came, not to mourn the passing of a compassionate king, but to seek assurance that Herod was dead , and that from him they had nothing more to fear.

Winds of jubilation swept the land of Judea. The brutal king was dead, and his remains deposited in the tomb at Herodium. Fearing retaliation from surviving members of

Herod's family, however, the Sanhedrin admonished, with little success, that the people exercise restraint in their celebration, fearing retribution from his heirs.

***

In the heart of Shira bas Haran there was no joy. The death of the vassal king brought only silent tears, sad reminders of the loss of her son Jabal at the behest of the deranged king. She would learn, sadly,, that Herod's legacy of evil had not gone with him to the grave, for his son Archelaus inherited the throne of Judea, keeping alive his father's vile reign.

Once again the heart of Judea was struck with terror. Archelaus, a weakling with

no ability to lead, sought strength in brutality even more heinous than that of his father. Archelaus had promised to release all political prisoners. Betrayal, however, was not long in coming. Any man he considered a threat to his power Archelaus dragged from the arms of his wife, often running him through on the spot in the presence of his weeping children. Some victims were sold into slavery, others suffered the agony of death in the stoning pit.

"Enemies of the crown!" Archelaus declared. "They deserve nothing better than death! Learn from this, Judea. The name of Herod shall not be dishonored!"

***

Romulo, viewing the rubble of an Archelaus rampage, grieved with a group of women whose men had been killed because they denied Archelaus's authority. Many villages were leveled by fire, their men beheaded, hanged, or hauled away in chains.

Romulo, longing to ease the suffering of the hollow-eyed women clutching their trembling, terrified children to their breasts, placed an arm across the slumping shoulders of a sobbing woman, assuring her that he and his men would bring no harm to her village.

A tearful young mother with a baby pleaded, "Please hold my son."

Taking the child in his arms, Romulo held him for a moment, then returned him to his mother.

"Thank you," she said. "Never again will he feel the arms of his father."

An older woman displayed a small coin. "It is all I have," she said, holding it out to Romulo. "Please, take it. I can do no less for Judea."

Romulo accepted the coin, and the woman responded with a tearful smile.

Climbing into the saddle, he instructed his men to distribute what food they carried, first to the children, then to their mothers.

Another woman caught his hand. "God go with you," she said.

"And with you."

He motioned the men to mount up and follow him into the hills west of the Jordan. A short distance from the village, a rider skidded his mount to a stop. "There's a Roman patrol up ahead," he said.

"How many?"Romulo said.

"Fifteen. Maybe twenty."

At Romulo's side, Varisias said, "They're probably from that outpost we spotted on the way here."

The rumble of iron-shod hooves alerted the rebels to the approach of the Roman patrol. At sight of the Judeans, however, the Romans abruptly reversed course and sped toward the safety of the outpost. The Judeans pursued at full gallop. The fleeing patrol reached the outpost, the gates swung open, and the Romans thundered through. Before the gates could close against them, the raging rebels swarmed into the compound.

Outnumbered by the rampaging patriots, the Romans mounted a desperate defense, but were no match for the storming Judeans. When the conflict was over, and the damage calculated, the rebels had sacked yet another Roman outpost.

Though not a major encounter, for the Jews it was a much needed victory.

Sitting his gray stallion, Romulo viewed with displeasure the blood-spattered residue: The bodies of young Romans, faces contorted, sprawled in unseeing, wide-eyed disbelief, who wanted as badly as he to live, but did what they were commanded. Smoldering mounds of ashes, gruesome monuments to the waste of war. He detested the look of it, the rancid odor, and the pain that it wrought.

His thoughts drifted back to the question of young Miletus: "Where will it lead?" Romulo asked himself, "Will it never end?"

Gone was the horrifying clash of metal against metal. Silenced were the frantic screams of the wounded and dying, the terrified scampers of riderless horses. No longer were heard the agonized groans, Judean blood mingling with Roman blood, neither distinguishable from the other. Lifeless faces displayed the surprise of having been felled by a blade which, except in the hands of an adversary, was a harmless piece of metal.

But Romulo knew this was not the hoped for end. He pondered for how much longer his rebel forces could hold out against the might of the Roman legions? The volunteers had fought valiantly, but, dedicated as they were to lifting the burden of oppression, rescuing Judea from the clutches of the pagans, his men had grown weary of war, longing to be at home with their wives and children.

Herod was gone, but his death had not ended the carnage. Following in his blood splattered footsteps he had left a ravaging maniac even more ruthless than himself.

Romulo's musings were interrupted by Judah. "The men are ready to move out, Romulo."

"Give the order."

At Judah's command, the patriots began herding horses out of the compound. Carts loaded with confiscated food and clothing creaked away, bound for the sanctuary of the Judean wilderness.

"There is a man–" Romulo said to Judah at his side, "a Bedouin chieftain named Amrak. Do you know of him?"

"Yes, I know of Amrak. My father used to speak of of him. Years ago Amrak sought my father's help in a war between desert tribes."

"And did your father oblige?"

"He did. What are you thinking?'

"I'm thinking we have a long ride ahead of us."

***

Deep into the Arabian desert rode Romulo, Judah and Zacheas with the sun at their backs. Romulo had calculated that only three riders would be less likely to attract a Roman patrol. Leaving Varisias in charge, he chose to accompany him the two men whose experience would be most beneficial: Zacheas for his sharp eyesight in the desert, and Judah because of his father's relationship to the desert chieftain Amrak.

As far as the eye could see, mounds of shimmering sand rose and fell, sculpted since time began by the swirling, torrid desert winds. In the distance a speck of darkness appeared on the horizon against the swirling gusts of white sand. Leaning forward in the saddle, Romulo squinted for a better look. "See that?" he said to Zacheas, riding beside him.

"I see it. Black goatskin tents. It's more than likely a Bedouin camp."

"How far?"

"Possibly an hour's ride."

Romulo said to Judah, "Did you hear that?"

"I heard," Judah said. "Zacheas is a good judge of time and distance. He calculates by the number of calluses on his backside."

Relieving the tension of a long hot ride, the sweaty, saddle-weary travelers shared a hearty laugh. By sunset they would reach the Bedouin camp.

***

With a sun baked hand Amrak bar Fahweh shaded his heavy brow. In one of countless desert clashes, he had lost his right eye to a blow from an enemy spear. A black-and-white striped kerchief covered what was left of the eye. Revered by his followers as a fearless warrior and courageous leader, Amrak was hardly five feet tall, carrying one hundred-forty pounds of tempered sinew. With the elders of his tribe, he stood with his back to the black goatskin tents, observing the approach of a small band of horsemen. Peering into the glittering sunset, he tried to determine whether the riders were friends or enemies. As they drew near he noted that they wore no tunics, no metal spiked helmets, and no cuirasses, which the Romans wore for protection against injury.

The riders' shadows reached the feet of the desert chieftain. Reining in their sweat-slick mounts, the man astride the gray stallion raised his right hand in a gesture of peace. In a strong, clear voice, he said, "I am Romulo de Vincius." With a sweep of his hand, he added, "These are my friends. We come in peace."

Amrak cast his elders a questioning look. Their stolid expressions admonished him to be wary of the strangers, for Romulo de Vincius was a Roman name.

Long ago the Romans had driven the nomads from

their water and grazing lands which, since the first sunrise, had been roamed by the Bedouin tribes seeking nourishment for their sheep and goats. As old as the desert sand was their suspicion of the Romans, for they had come, not in peace, but to conquer.

Amrak recognized Romulo's language as Aramaic, which he understood but seldom spoke, preferring the Greek or Hebrew dialects commonly spoken among the tribes. Struggling to form an intelligent response to Romulo's greeting, he said, "For what purpose have you come?"

"We come seeking the counsel of the desert chieftain Amrak," said Romulo.

Amrak accepted as assent the silent nods of the elders. "I am Amrak," he said. With a wave of his hand, he invited the riders to dismount and come forward. They did so, leading their mounts.

At Amrak's feet glowed an open fire of dried camel dung. Over the bed of coals simmered a cauldron of lamb stew, its enticing aroma tantalizing the nostrils of the hungry wayfarers.

To Amrak, Romulo said, "We are Judean patriots. We have come to ask your help."

Since the dawn of time a plea for help from one in need had revealed the weakness of strong men, offering help to one in need. Even tyrants, highwaymen, and nomadic, battle scarred warriors such as Amrak bar Fahweh, had been known to crumble under the weight of such entreaties. Bound by tradition were the tribes, who turned away no one.

Still, the desert chieftain was not one to be deceived by the devious Romans.

"How are we to know, Romulo de Vincius," Amrak said, "that you and your friends
are not spies for the enemy?"

"That you do not, wise Amrak," said Romulo, seeking

the eyes of the burly tribesmen eying him with dubious stares. "But, only a fool would attempt to deceive a man of the stature of Amrak bar Fahweh."

For a moment longer the gaze of the desert sheik rested upon the swarthy face of the man with a Roman name who claimed to be a Judean patriot.

"We come," Romulo said, "in the name of Hezekiah of Galilee."

Amrak's dubious expression faded, his face glowing with pleasure at the mention of his Galilean friend. "Hezekiah?" he said.

"Yes. His son Judah fights beside the Judean rebels, and has come with us to greet you."

"Judah? Son of Hezekiah?"

Judah stepped forward. "I am Judah," he said. "My father often spoke of you."

"Spoke?" said Amrak with a furrowed brow.

"My father died resisting the Roman domination in Galilee."

Amrak placed a hand of welcome on the shoulder of Judah ben Hezekiah. To Romulo, he said, "You are welcome here, Romulo de Vincius—you and your friends. The time will come, however, when a Judean patriot must explain why he bears the name of a Roman infidel.

Meanwhile, you honor my tent with your presence, and if there is something I can do in memory of the great Hezekiah, I will be deeply pleased." He spread his arms, indicating the cauldron of steaming stew. "Now, you must be hungry. Please, come, eat."

A word here, a gesture there from Amrak, and long-robed women with veiled faces

hastened to serve food and wine to the famished travelers, joining their host and his elders, seated with crossed ankles around the fire.

Beyond the circle of tents, the squawking of restless camels filtered through the rhythmic beat of stringed instruments and goatskin drums. Amrak clapped his hands and four young women appeared, gyrating in time with the music.

Both Arabs and Jews descended from Father Abraham, the one from his outcast son Ishmael, the other from the favored Isaac. For countless centuries a bitter rivalry had festered between the two proud peoples, but the warmth of Amrak's hospitality exemplified the tradition of the desert nomads that even strangers be welcomed to their tents.

"How fortunate that you should arrive at this time," said Amrak, "for a mistitha is planned, and our hope is that you will abide with us until then."

Eager as Romulo was to get to the business for which he had endured days of scorching

desert heat, to decline the Bedouin hospitality would be an insult to his gracious host. Also, his Judean volunteers, in whose behalf he came seeking the aid of the desert chieftain, were ill equipped to continue the freedom fight alone. His journey into the desert was to secure the battle strength of Amrak's warriors to challenge the might of the Roman legions.

Though the vagaries of war were not deterred by the joy of tribal festivities, Romulo responded with a smiling face."To attend a marriage of your people." he said, "would be an honor beyond measure."

***

For three days and three nights Romulo waited, while all around him the air came alive with laughter, music, singing and dancing. Food, a vital component of Arab family functions, was served endlessly from sundown to sundown. Women from the bride's family displayed zaabaah comprised of her clothes, gifts from the groom's family, and other items of adoration for the bride-to-be.

Arab tradition dictated that the bride and groom not

meet until after the wedding ceremony. Perched on a houdach, a saddle made especially for the occasion, the bride must arrive at the groom's tent aboard a camel.

Sundown of the fourth day marked the conclusion of the marriage festivities. Amrak raised his arms toward the tent of the bride and groom, giving them his blessing. "The celebration of this day," he said, "shall continue for as long as these two shall live. May Allah fill their tent with love, and walk with them to eternal happiness."

And the people said, "Allah be praised."

***

In the Bedouin culture coffee was more than a social pleasantry. It was a ritual, the height of hospitality, a delicacy resulting from a meticulous process: Above an open fire an iron skillet was suspended. In the skillet were placed coffee beans, stirred with a long-handled ladle to ensure proper roasting. Once the roasting process was complete the beans were cooled in a decorative wooden container, after which they were ground into a granular substance. The grains were then poured into a copper pot filled with water, boiled three times before the greenish, unsweetened coffee could be served.

Amrak drained the last drop of the brew from his earthenware cup, stroking his lips with his fingertips, savoring the last drop of the delicate brew, and wiped them on the front of his robe. He then turned his attention to Romulo, seated with the circle of elders around the eternal flame.

"What is it," Amrak said, "that Romulo de Vincius seeks from his friends?"

The leathery faces leaned toward Romulo, piercing eyes seeking his, sharp ears tuned to his response.

"I am a Roman," Romulo said, and the faces around the fire shrank from the repugnance of his admission.

"We know that," said Amrak. "No self respecting Jew would allow himself to be called by a Roman name."

"But, I am a Jew," said Romulo, and again the faces leaned forward. "I was born in Rome of Jewish parents. I make no attempt to deceive you. In my early years I was fascinated by the pomp and pageantry of the Roman legion. I dreamed of one day becoming a part of it. Then, after my parents were imprisoned and tortured for refusing to recognize Caesar as a god,

I wanted to destroy him and all his Roman empire. Even so, I believed that my hope of escaping the fate of my parents was to become a soldier in the Roman army, where Jews were not welcome.

"Then, when I was seventeen, I saved from drowning the son of a Roman senator. Out of gratitude for my having done so, and aware of my ambition, the senator arranged for me to adopt his family name, and I became Romulo de Vincius.

"Accepted into the legion, every day for five years, from sunrise to sunset, I trained with my unit, learning discipline, self control, and how to kill. In time, the horror of my parents' death began to fade, and I became proud to be a Roman soldier, willing at any time to sacrifice my life for Caesar. And then–" He paused, taking a deep breath.

"Yes?" said Amrak.

"You must know of Herod's decree," Romulo said, noting the lowering of eyes, and the exchange of knowing glances among the elders. "When the vassal of Rome ordered the massacre of the male children, I was no longer proud to be a Roman soldier, serving with the blind loyalty demanded by the emperor. My efforts to resign my commission were futile. I then chose to desert the legion, for which the penalty is death."

As he talked, a rider couched his small, fawn-colored camel and dismounted beyond the fire. With a slight nod, he motioned to Amrak.

The sheik joined him outside the circle, drew the rider aside, and leaned close to listen. The rider cast a furtive glance at Romulo. Not convinced that Romulo had come on a mission of peace, the rider mounted his camel, glancing warily over his shoulder as he rode away.

Amrak returned to the circle around the fire and, with a steady gaze, surveyed the expectant faces. A dozen pairs of questioning eyes awaited his report.

"A Roman patrol is camped less than an hour's ride from where we sit," Amrak said, pinning Romulo with a stare. "It is his belief that you brought them here. What say you, Romulo de Vincius?"

Romulo felt the stab of defeat, his insides stricken by failure.

For eight hundred years Israel had suffered the control of aggressive powers such as Assyria, Babylonia, Persia, Egypt, and now the detested Romans. Having led the Roman patrol to the Bedouin camp, Romulo feared that he had squandered all hope of enlisting the aid of Amrak and his desert warriors in the struggle to free Judea from the shackles of foreign oppression.

Amrak's steady gaze demanded a response. "What say you, Romulo de Vincius?"

Romulo took a moment to formulate the words he wanted his host to hear. "There is no heart heavier than mine," he said, "if I have brought a threat upon the tent of noble Amrak. You have treated my friends and me with honor. We have shared your food, drunk your wine, and enjoyed the blessings bestowed upon you by your god Allah. And before our God Jehovah, I assure you that I had no knowledge of the Roman patrol. They would follow me only because they want to see me dead."

Weighing the words of him who came seeking their help, the eyes of the solemn faces around the circle sought each other.

"My countrymen," Romulo said, "rebelled against

Herod, and so against Caesar. And now we're faced with the tyranny and brutality of Archelaus. Though our numbers are smaller, and our supplies limited, we fight on, dedicated to a cause we believe is just.

"You too have suffered the denigrating demands of a ruthless regime. We have come to ask your help against the pagan hordes, to restore to our peoples the freedom and dignity they have been denied. We are here for no other purpose."

***

Dismissed by Amrak while the elders deliberated, Romulo, Judah, and Zacheas were provided the finest quarters, wine in endless supply, and an abundance of food, Burly tribesmen bearing metal-tipped lances stationed themselves at the door of their tent, serving their needs, and protecting them from evil until the elders' arrived at their decision.

Treated as honored guests, the three were free to move about the village, enjoying the hospitality of Arab tradition. Even so, Romulo would have traded his host's gracious amenities for one positive answer. Yet, any attempt to expedite the deliberation of the elders would be fruitless, perceived by them with suspicion as an attempt to influence their deliberation. When the proper time arrived, Romulo would be summoned to join them around the fire to be told of the result of their counsel.

Mid-afternoon of the fourth day a white-turbaned guard stuck his head in the doorway of Romulo's tent. "Romulo de Vincius," said he, "you will come with me."

Romulo followed him to the campfire where Amrak sat surrounded by a dozen members of the tribal council. Hooded in checkered headdress against the blistering sun, they fixed their dark, questioning eyes on the face of Romulo de Vincius.

"The Roman patrol," Amrak announced without further comment, "is no longer a matter of concern. And your cause, Romulo de Vincius, has been verified by our people. As we would honor one of our own, we now honor you."

Having spent days in a state of uncertainty, Romulo allowed himself to relax and observe the ritual which he knew would follow. Amrak extended his right hand palm up over the flame. With a nod, he invited Romulo to place his right hand, palm down, on his own. Amrak then placed his left hand on top of Romulo's right, and Romulo covered Amrak's with his left hand. As a gesture of commitment among men of honor, the elders then leaned in and placed their hands on Romulo's.

"For as long as the flame of memory has glowed," Amrak said, "there has been bloodshed between the Arab and the Jew. Many wars have been fought, the reasons for them long since forgotten. You, Romulo de Vincius, though we all descend from the seeds of father Abraham, you as the sons of Isaac, and we as the sons of Ishmael the outcast. But we now are bound–Jew and Arab–by a common need, to free ourselves from the tyranny of Rome, and from the heinous crimes of the blood-thirsty Archelaus. From the smallest spark rages the greatest fire, and you, Romulo de Vincius, have rekindled in the hearts of my people the flame of hope and pride from which we call upon Allah to free your people from the bonds of degradation."

And the voices around the fire chorused, "Allah be praised."

CHAPTER 15

Atop the rampart surrounding the Roman outpost, Major Cassio scanned the endless expanse of bare, colorless desert, seeing nothing, except for mounds of windswept sand, stretching eastward as far as the beginning of time. He wrapped his arms around his body against the early evening chill flowing in off the desert, reminded once again of how much he hated garrison duty. Though he considered himself superior to the crude Herod, in the service of the king, Cassio had languished in the luxury of the palace where he answered directly to Herod himself. After Archelaus inherited the throne, demoting the major from his privileged status, stripping the major of his position of privilege.

The throne of Judea was a familial gift from his father Herod, but Archelaus was nonetheless beholden to Augustus Caesar, of whom he requested, and was granted, the freedom of choosing his palace staff. Aware of the loathing with which the supercilious Cassio had regarded his father Herod, Archelaus relegated the major to the status of commander of the garrison, far beyond the copious bustle of the city of Jerusalem.

Cassio, with no experience in armed conflict, was sickened by the sight of blood, with no desire to risk shedding any of his own. Robbed by Archelaus of the luxury of the king's palace, Cassio considered appealing to Rome, protesting distaste for his new, undesirable assignment. In view of the emperor's rebuff in their last encounter, however, Cassio deemed an appeal fruitless. So it was with considerable repugnance that he assumed his duties at the outpost.

Rumors of a rebel build up had circulated for days, but Cassio had seen no sign of such activity, and saw none now, his patrols having reported no extraordinary activity in the desert to the east. He, therefore, dismissed the rumors as a groundless attempt by the hapless Jews to bolster their courage against Roman odds.

Weary of peering into the barren nothingness of the desert, thoughts of retiring to the comfort of his quarters filled Cassio's head when, suddenly– There! On the horizon, a reed-thin line of darkness–extending along the sandy crest seemingly forever. Like a swarm of locusts, the closer it came, the larger, more intense it grew.

Major Cassio did not deceive himself that what he saw moving deliberately toward the outpost was a swarm of locusts. Squinting, he could make out the forms of arms and heads, heads of men, men on camels and horses, sweeping in from the desert. Hundreds, maybe thousands, of men bearing lances, slings, and bows. Like the creeping devastation of molten lava they shortened the distance between themselves and Cassio's Roman outpost.

Fearful of an attack by the ever widening shadow, Cassio trembled with fright.

"Centurions!" he shouted in a shrill voice. "Ready your units!"

"Battle stations!" the centurions ordered, and

legionaries scrambled to their defensive positions along the wall.

"Ready arms!'

It was impossible to determine whether the oncoming forces were Jews."But," Cassio sneered, "who else would defend the cause of the bedraggled Judeans?"

Over the crest and across the desert sands the riders steadily approached the citadel.

A lone horseman burst into the open and pulled up beyond the range of the Roman archers. Cassio, peering over the wall, heard the rider shout, "Major Marcus Cassio!"

The rider paused for a response from the wall, but heard none. "Are you there, Major?"

"I am Major Cassio," came the tentative reply.

"Major Cassio," said the horseman, "my commander, Captain Romulo de Vincius, requests that you and your men lay down your arms and surrender in the name of our God Jehovah!"

"Romulo, eh?" Cassio jeered with more bravado than he felt. "So, the traitor pits his God against the might of Rome." He took another look at the gathering force a hundred yards from where he crouched behind the wall. What he saw was a fighting force even larger and stronger than it had appeared moving in from the desert. Were those Bedouin lined up out there on the side of the Jews? In the deepening shadows it was difficult to tell.

Yes! A closer look revealed hordes of desert warriors on horses and camels, armed with spears and short knives! Cassio clung to the wall to support his shaken body. Finally he mustered the courage to threaten, "An army whose only hope is an invisible God is an army that begs to be destroyed."

"Is that your answer, major?" the horseman called back.

Cassio hesitated He was not ready to risk annihilation

by the Bedouin warriors lined up against him. He searched for the hated Romulo, finding him at the head of the assembled masses. Then, grasping at the only straw left to him, he invested what remained of his arrogance in a feeble declaration that he hoped would deter the rebel onslaught.

"Those whose position is hopeless," he said, "are denied the privilege of dictating the terms of battle. Bring on your God!"

Spinning his mount about, the rider delivered the message to Romulo.

With Amrak at his side, and Jewish patriots and Bedouin warriors lined up behind him, Romulo shouted, "Ready the lancers!"

"Lancers ready!" Varisias said.

"Ready bowmen and slingers!"

"Bowmen and slingers ready!" Judah responded.

"Ready hooks and ladders," Romulo ordered. "We scale the wall!"

Romulo stabbed the air with his sword and spurred the gray toward the enemy bastion. To the ear-shattering blast of the ram's horn, he led his charges into battle.

Roman arrows, lances, and catapulted stones filled the air,while the patriots and Amrak's warriors cleared the wall, dispatching the defenders atop the ramparts. They swarmed up the ladders and over the wall, screaming war cries, swinging swords, and flinging lances that found their marks. Judean and Bedouin fighting side-by-side, they swept over the Roman contingent, putting the torch to tents and huts.

Against the smoldering background, Romulo viewed the destruction, savoring the victory, and silently praising his men for their assault on another Roman outpost.

"Aye, Romulo!"

The voice came from behind him. Many months had passed since he last heard it, but Major Marcus Cassio's supercilious voice was unmistakable. With a sardonic smile, Romulo faced his old nemesis crouching against the wall, huddling inside his arms, trying to insulate himself from the contact he abhorred..

Romulo had presumed him dead in the melee."So," said he, "the rats come to feed on the flesh of the dead."

"Romulo!" the Roman screamed crazily.

"How did you escape death here where heroes come to die?"

"I give you warning, Romulo, you will lie among them!"

"Warning, major? You whose greatest achievements have been murdering old men and little children. You would give me warning?"

"You traitor! You deserter!" Cassio screamed. "I swore I would find you!"

"And find me you have."

"We will kill you!" Cassio's shrill voice threatened. "We will kill you!"

"We, major? And where are the others? All who might help you, lie finished in defeat."

Cassio glanced about, frantically seeking help from comrades. Discovering that he was the only Roman left alive, he scrambled to his feet, and scampered up a ladder to escape the wrath of the pursuing Judean.

Romulo, close on his heels, grabbed the fleeing Roman's ankles, flung him to the ground, and pinned him on his back. Whipping out his dagger, with its point he pricked the throat of the terrified major.

Accompanied by half a dozen Bedouin tribesmen, Amrak said, "What say you, Romulo?"

"Amrak!" Romulo said. "I have a prize for you." He got to his feet and pulled Cassio up with him. "A prisoner, Amrak. Major Marcus Cassio of the Roman legion, who would have my head."

"Perhaps, my friend," said Amrak, "we will have instead the head of the careless major. In the desert we have a special treatment for such as he." He regarded the trembling Cassio with a villainous eye. "First we stake him out on his back in the sand. Then we mount upon a rod above his forehead a skin of cool water. The water drips upon the head of the major, and drives him mad long before he dies of thirst, hunger, and the heat of the desert sun."

Romulo relaxed his grip, releasing the hysterical Cassio to the Bedouin warriors.

"No, please!" Cassio begged. "I will do anything! I have great riches from the coffers of Herod. Anything!"

Romulo and Amrak watched the screaming Roman being dragged away. He gave his head a solemn shake as he faced the desert chieftain.

Amrak displayed a wry smile. How many times had he viewed with sadness the carnage of battle, counting the dead of friend and foe? And to how many anxious wives and weeping mothers had he reported the death of a cherished one whom they had expected to see riding safely home before nightfall?

"For now, friend Romulo," said he, "for now we have won. But, we know, don't we, that the Romans cannot abide anything short of total victory? They can afford only to win, and will do whatever is necessary to accomplish that. If they lose Judea, they lose their stranglehold on the rest of the world, for, if defeated by the patriots of their smallest province, the humiliation would be too great for them to bear."

"Then," said Romulo, "what is the alternative to defeat?"

"We, like the Romans, are dedicated to our cause. But our cause is different from theirs. We seek freedom, while they want only to dominate. We are as stubborn as they. But the difference is–"

"Yes?"

"The difference is that they have the manpower, the equipment, the experience–the means of war in unlimited supply, and they don't need a reason for killing. To them conflict is a way of life."

Romulo heard his own thoughts in the words in the words of the desert chieftain.. "What then?" he said. "We can't give up because we fear defeat."

"In the eyes of my men," said Amrak, "I see the look that tells me they have seen enough of fighting."

Romulo had seen the same longing in the eyes of his own men, wishing he could assure them that one day they would celebrate the joy of victory.

"But, they won't quit," Romulo said.

"We will never quit!" Amrak shot back. "And we do not give up. We fight on because we are stronger in spirit than the Roman mercenaries. They need not be strong because they are many. Reduce their number to ours and they will not oppose us, for their only reward is conquest and control."

Romulo looked out across the colorless plain beyond the mounds of death. "What then is our reward for fighting on?" he said.

The old warrior stood in silence. Looking back. Counting the times. Counting the dead. Recalling the pain, the bloodshed, the uselessness of war, war that had been thrust upon him by the demands of his culture, his country, and his god.

"A babe is born, a boy grows, and a man learns," said Amrak, "and at the peak of his learning he dies. And those who suffer his loss shed tears for him." He paused, sliding a gnarled hand over his sun-leathered face. "That is our reward, friend Romulo. The tears of our women and children." Again he said, "That is our reward."

From the west rose the ear-shattering blast of a Roman trumpet, the sound of thundering hoof beats bearing down on the outpost! The rumble grew louder nearing the garrison.

"Stand fast!" Romulo barked. "Varisias, Judah, ready

your units!"

But it was too late, and there were too few patriots to withstand the mounted onslaught of the galloping Romans pouring into the fort.

Romulo felt the sting of a lance in his chest. Bleeding from the gash, he fell to the ground, yanked the lance free, and lay still. Iron shod boots raced past, leaving him for dead. Thirty feet away he spotted his gray stallion and wondered if he could make it that far. He had no choice. He had to try. Flattening himself on the ground, he began pulling himself forward, weaving his laborious way around fallen comrades. Finally, he was able to get close enough to grab a stirrup.

Like a vise Romulo felt a hand clamped around his wrist. Shocked, he stared into the face of a spike-helmeted Roman. The Roman caught him by the shoulders and helped him to his feet. "Do you want to kill me?" said the Roman.

Romulo shook his head. "No," he said.

"Then I will not kill you." Helping Romulo into the saddle, he slapped the stallion on the rump, and said, "Go in peace—Romulo."

CHAPTER 16

Shimmering orange and gold fingers of the rising sun reached for the gray, low-lying hills of Judea. Only the throaty alarm of the cock's crow, and the bleating of hungry sheep anxious to be led to pasture disturbed the early morning silence embracing the modest home of Simon ben Haada. For Simon it was his favorite time of day. From childhood he was taught to rise early, promising himself that the sun would never rise before he did. Each day began with the solemn ritual, "Hear, O Israel, the Lord God, the Lord is One–"

This morning his meditation was interrupted by the muffled clop-clop of a horse's hooves on dry, barren soil. Simon stepped outside his door where his seventy-year-old eyes fell upon the unhurried approach of a gray stallion carrying a saddle with no rider. He combed his yellowing beard with fingers twisted by age, pondering why a horse with no rider would make its way to his doorstep. He reached out, and the horse responded with a gentle nicker. Moving his hand along the horse's sweaty neck, under the long flowing mane to the withers, he struck something sticky. Inspecting his fingers, he was not surprised to find them stained with blood. It was not the first time he had encountered a wounded soldier. Simon knew what he had to do.

"Joshua," he called.

From the manger emerged a youth of twelve whose smile evinced an eagerness to be of service to his grandfather. "Yes, grandfather?" said the lad

"Joshua, somewhere there is a man without a horse." Simon spoke without haste, but in his voice Joshua detected a note of urgency.

"That is not uncommon in this time, sir," said the youth.

Simon spread his hand, exposing the blood stains. 'I found this at the withers," he said. "It is not yet dry."

The gray stallion's long mane, as opposed to the short-cropped Arabian blacks preferred by the Romans, told Simon this horse was not the mount of a legionary.

"The man who rode this horse," he said, "may still be alive and in need of help."

"Yes, grandfather."

"Bring the ox from the manger, my son, and yoke him to the cart. We must see if we can find the man whose blood the horse carries."

The boy did as he was told. Simon tethered the gray to a sapling, climbed onto the two-wheeled cart, and took up the reins.

"We must hurry," Simon said, "lest he suffer too long."

They set off in search of an injured warrior, as they had often done in recent times.

"The horse came from the south, grandfather?"

"Yes, along the Herodium road."

Urging the plodding ox forward, Simon scanned the byways for sight of a wounded warrior.

"Perhaps he was attacked by highwaymen," said Joshua.

"Perhaps," said Simon, thinking beyond that probability. He suspected it was more likely that the man was injured in the attack near Herodium of which he heard talk at the synagogue last night.

Simon glanced from one side of the narrow cart path to the other.

"Watch closely on your side," he said to Joshua, "and I'll watch on mine. We must be especially watchful among the rocks and bushes."

A short time later the boy called out, "Look, grandfather! There!" He pointed to a clump of evergreens. "A scrap of cloth!"

Simon halted the cart and hurried to where he found the brown cloth clinging to the shrubbery. He grabbed it up and searched it for blood stains. "Ah!" he said, at sight of the red smears. "Well done, Joshua. He can't be far away."

Each of them went off in a different direction, searching the dry underbrush and sandstone mounds. Only a few minutes passed before Simon heard an ear-splitting scream from Joshua. Simon moved quickly into a small ravine and found his grandson in the grasp of a wild-eyed man, his chest wrapped in a crude bandage. Fashioned from his brown cloak, Simon suspected.

With the point of a dagger the man nudged Joshua's throat."Don't come any closer," he threatened as Simon came near, "or the boy will die."

"We only want to help you," Simon said.

"Get back!" the man screamed, maddened by the pain wracking his body.

"Please," Simon said. "We mean no harm. Let us help you to safety."

"Stay away!" His eyes rolled back, his head lolling to one side.

"Stay–" The dagger fell from his hand, and Joshua

squirmed free of the unconscious warrior's grasp.

"Onto the cart with him, Joshua," said Simon.

Together they dragged and lifted the limp body onto the ox cart. Simon removed his cloak and placed it over the head of the wounded passenger to protect him from the already scorching sun. Simon flailed the ox with a hempen lash, fearing that help for the wounded man might come too late.

From beneath the cloak came a hoarse whisper. "Shira."

Simon and Joshua exchanged concerned looks, each questioning whether the other had heard. Simon motioned his grandson to lean closer.

Joshua lifted the cloak from the man's face and heard him whisper, "In the village." His head moved feverishly from side to side. "In the village. Shira," he said, sinking again into unconsciousness.

"Run ahead, my son," Simon said. "You can get there ahead of the ox."

Joshua leaped from the cart and raced along the narrow pathway.

"Take the horse," his grandfather called.

Mounting the gray, Joshua raced at a hard gallop to Bethlehem, searching for a woman of whom he knew nothing, except her name, Shira.

A hurried inquiry of a man in the village–"Shira? Yes. You're almost there"–sent him to the door of Shira bas Haran.

"I am Joshua," he told her when she answered his call. "My grandfather and I found a wounded man along the road from Herodium. We don't know who he is, but he called your name. He rode a gray horse."

A gray horse. Shira's immediate thought was of Romulo. She snatched up a mantle and covered her head. "Please take me to him," she said.

"Do you ride?" Joshua asked.

"I have no horse."

"Then you must ride with me." Joshua held out his hand and helped her up behind him.

"Put your arms around my waist," he said, and she did so.

The last time she was on a horse she had struggled to free herself of the boorish Quintas. Not a pleasant recollection."Is this the horse of the wounded rider?" she said.

"Yes, we believe so. Do you know it?"

Except for a solemn nod, she made no answer.

Joshua urged the horse along the cobblestone street.

Shira directed him to the home of the village physician, Reuben ben Ashur. "Please come," she said to the doctor. "For this the Lord will surely bless you."

"Yes," Reuben said with a patient nod of his balding gray head. Often these days, with so many to care for, the blessing of the Lord had been his only reward. Even so, he gathered up what he would need to treat a wounded man, tossed his bag into his ox cart, and joined Joshua and Shira in their haste to reach the home of Simon ben Haada.

The gray stallion told Shira who she would find there. She knelt beside the straw pallet, reaching out to the unconscious warrior. "Romulo!" she whispered.

Recognizing the name of the rebel leader, Simon and Joshua exchanged silent looks.

Reuben also knew then who his patient was, but kept busy inspecting his wounds."Hot water," the doctor ordered. "Lots of hot water, and clean cloths for the wound."

Simon brought the water and cloths, handing them to Shira. "Swab the wound for me," Reuben said to Shira. "Gently now."

Except for Romulo's labored breathing, Shira saw no sign of life. Her heart went out to him, a Judean with a Roman name, whom she once hated, but whom she could no longer hate.

"More water!" Reuben shouted, struggling to save the life of a man he did not know, but whose name he recognized. Romulo de Vincius, leader of the Judean patriots! "We're almost finished."

CHAPTER 17

Through long nights of silence and days of uncertainty, Shira hardly left Romulo's side.

Simon had laid a pallet for her on the floor beside the wounded warrior. Often in the night she awoke to bathe his wounds, change the bandages as Reuben had instructed, giving him nourishment in his rare periods of consciousness. Sometimes he would grasp her hand as though afraid she might leave him.

With caring fingertips, she caressed the face of the man, once strong and vibrant, who took her son away. Jabal would be almost three now, vital in his formative years, she mused, even as she feared that Romulo's life was slipping away. She prayed for his recovery, not for herself only, but for Judea. Without Romulo, who would lead the rebels in their fight for freedom?

She felt Simon's gaze upon her. Her eyes met his, seeking the answer to a question that many times she had asked herself "Can we win, Simon?" she said.

The old man tugged at his beard. "Those of us who

follow the will of the Lord have won already. Still, I fear that the chances of a rebel victory over the pagan hordes are quite limited. Your Romulo, however, has shown great skill as a leader of men. He has made the Romans aware that the spirit of Judea is to resist with all our strength. Our greatest hope is our trust in God, who has promised to send a messiah who will rule the world."

"How long must we wait?"

"Until the Lord is ready. It is not ours to question the ways of the Lord. We can only trust his covenant, and await the coming of the Deliverer." With a curious cock of his gray head, he said, "Perhaps when we are ready to receive him, the messiah will come."

Romulo was dying. Shira knew it, and Reuben ben Ashur, without a spoken word, confirmed it days ago. First Ezlon, she mused, then her parents, and then Jabal had been taken from her. And now, cradling Romulo's head on her lap as she knelt beside him, she knew that soon again she would suffer the loss of someone dear. Wishing for a friend with whom she could share her sorrow, she longed for Hannah, from whom she had been separated for much too long.

Romulo had not spoken for days, but suddenly one morning she was startled at the sound of his hoarse voice. "I must go to them," he wheezed. "Now, more than ever they need me. Varisias, Judah, that boy Zacheas– I must– And Amrak–"

Romulo had not been told that his friends perished in the battle at Herodium. She had heard that Judah survived, but she knew nothing of his whereabouts. Amrak also died in the onslaught, though many of his warriors escaped to the desert.

Romulo, his body weak and emaciated, at last became resigned to the reality of his last days. He asked Shira to bring his dagger and scabbard. When she held them out to him, he took the dagger, inspecting it for the last time, as though saying goodbye to an old friend.

"Take this–to Judah," he said with a wracking cough. "It belongs to him now."

In his pleading eyes she read the question that only she could answer: Had she accepted him as the Jew that he was? Had she forgiven him for taking her son away?

"Yes, Romulo," she whispered, placing her face close to his. "As you have been taught to be proud, I have been taught to forgive."

He grasped her hand and drew her closer. "Shira," he gasped. Then, with his last breath, he shouted, "Shira!" His body convulsed, and he lay still.

Shira wrapped him in a strong embrace, loving him more in death than she had allowed herself to love him while he lived.

Romulo's mission was now hers.

***

Into the wilderness Shira urged the gray stallion. Tucked inside her robe was the dagger that the dying Romulo instructed her to deliver to Judah ben Hezekiah. The badge of authority, the torch of leadership, would now pass to the Galilean.

Quiet engulfed the countryside in the eerie time before night became day, silence broken only by the distant sounds of lowing cattle and bleating sheep. An occasional candle-lit window bolstered her courage, reassuring her that she was not alone in the world, even while she felt more alone than ever before. Ezlon was gone, Jabal was gone, and now Romulo was gone. And God seemed far away

Drawing her robe close against the early morning chill, she was lost in thoughts of the past. Almost she could feel Romulo's arms drawing her to him in a strong embrace, lamenting the loss of so much time that they could have spent together. Rather than betray her memory of Ezlon, except for one too brief moment, she had denied herself the freedom to love and be loved by the repentant Romulo.

She gave the horse his head, letting him pick his way over limestone hills and tangled masses of greenery clinging to the ravine walls. In search of the rebel camp which Romulo had described, she trusted the horse to find his way up the draw that he had climbed many times before with Romulo astride him, toward a break in the rocks leading to a clearing. She was challenged by a bowman who demanded to know who she was, and why she was there.

"I am Shira bas Haran," she said. "I bring news from your leader, Romulo de Vincius."

A young man who told her he was Ezekiel, escorted her to the campsite where he introduced her to the assembled rebels seated in groups around camp fires.

Atop Romulo's gray stallion, Shira surveyed the questioning faces of those who had escaped death at Herodium. Even so, in their eyes she sensed discouragement, disappointment, that told her they had come near to giving up.

"I bring greetings from your leader Romulo," she said in a loud voice, "who lies in a secret place, suffering wounds inflicted by the pagans in the battle of Herodium."

"He's lucky to be there," grumbled a man nearby.

"Well said," his neighbor agreed.

"He's better off than we are," said a third, "holed up here, waiting for death by the pagans."

Shira cast Ezekiel a questioning glance. He shrugged with a dubious shake of his head."They're about ready to give up," he said. "Some have discarded their weapons and gone home. Only Romulo could spur them to action. Maybe when he comes back–"

Only Shira knew Romulo would not be coming back. She spread her arms for quiet."Please, hear me," she pleaded. "I am here only because Romulo could not come.

He urges you to not lose heart. The cause of Judea is too great. You must fight on!"

"We don't know you."

"You say you come from Romulo. How do we know that?"

"You know the horse I ride is Romulo's.," she said. "And I have brought his–"

From somewhere in the crowd she heard an authoritative voice."I know this woman!"

Angry voices fell silent, and the men gave way for Judah ben Hezekiah who came riding out of their midst. Piercing eyes followed the tall Galilean as he pulled up beside Shira. He greeted her with a nod and a half smile.

"If you know me," he said to the gathering, "you know this woman. If you know Romulo, you know this woman. If you know yourselves, you know this woman." Solemnly he scanned the crowd. Then, in a quiet voice, he said, "Her son Jabal was one of those innocents slain by the maniacal Herod. If you would reject this woman, then you must also reject the cause of Judea."

A wave of murmured protests swept the assemblage.

"If Judah says it–"

"Yes, but he's a Galilean."

"What does he care about us?"

"You must not speak so!" Shira cried. "Listen to me, men of Judea. You are our only hope. You who have fought and bled and suffered for the sake of our fathers, and for our children. Without you, we are lost."

"We're lost already."

"Please, listen! Judea is counting on you. Your wives and your children–they are praying for you. And God himself is counting on you to keep up the fight."

"Where is he now?"

"Where is the God who promises so much and delivers so little?"

"God is God!" Shira shouted above the din. "He is

where he is, and we cannot question his ways. He dwells with those who believe in him." At the top of her voice, she said, "There is no place in Judea for non-believers! Who helped us escape the bonds of Egyptian slavery? Who guided the feet of Moses who led us through the wilderness to the Promised Land? Who brought us back from Babylon to the land of our fathers?"

She studied the hollow eyes of those who heard, fearing that her entreaties had fallen on closed ears. Then, from a timid voice nearby she heard someone murmur, "God did."

"God did!' she echoed strongly.

"God did," another agreed. "Bless his holy name."

Then rose an eerie chorus of voices which a moment before were angry and accusing. With increasing velocity, mounting to a powerful crescendo, she heard a chorus of, "God did! God did! God did! Bless his holy name!"

A strange smile worked its way across the bearded face of Judah ben Hezekiah. Ezekiel shook his head in disbelief.

"And he will do it again!" Shira assured them. "The enemies of Judea are camped but a short distance from where we are. I go to meet them! Will you go with me?"

To a man the full-throated response was, "We will go with you!"

Shira knew nothing of battle, but, strengthened by the renewed eagerness of the men who revered Romulo, she was ready to lead his beleaguered warriors into battle against the hated Romans.

Judah reined in beside her. Drawing a saber from its saddle scabbard he held it out to her hilt first. "Take this." he said. "You may need it to stay alive."

"I know nothing of weapons," she said, immediately recalling the contorted face of Colonel Marius whose belly she had punctured with his own dagger.

Judah responded with a thin smile. "I know that, and you know that," said he."But the men don't know that.

They will follow more readily if they see you wielding a weapon. And you will learn quickly."

Still wary of carrying the sword, she gave her head a dubious shake. It appeared so massive.

"I would wager," Judah said, "that never before have you inflamed the passions of farmers, shepherds, beggars, and shopkeepers to challenge the forces of Rome."

She grasped the hilt of the sword with both hands and held it aloft. She was surprised that it was not as heavy as it had appeared.

"Romulo would be proud of you," said Judah.

"Romulo is dead."

Judah was stunned. "Dead? Romulo?"

"Two days ago, from his wounds at Herodium." she said. "The men need not know yet." From beneath her robe she drew Romulo's short sword in the silver scabbard and thrust it into Judah's hand. "He wanted you to have this," she said.

"Romulo's sword," he said. "I will cherish this as a part of my friend." He then tucked the dagger inside his sash. "The men are waiting," he said.

With the rebels' screeching battle cry, Shira stabbed the air with the sword and spurred the gray into a dead run, leading her charges into battle. War cries, accompanied by the blaring ram's horn, encouraged by the power of a fresh new voice, the rebels raced toward the Roman outpost on the plain.

"Take no chances with your life!" Judah admonished Shira above the roar of hoof beats. "Judea needs you!"

The rebels scampered up the ladders, scaled the walls of the garrison, engaging the Romans in fierce hand-to-hand combat. They slashed and jabbed with such ferocity that the Romans were soon overrun. And Shira savored for the first time the taste of victory.

There was no time for celebrating.

At the discretion of Augustus Caesar, Archelaus served

as tetrarch, not king, of Judea. Even so, the blood-thirsty son of Herod was eager to prove that he could rule with as strong a hand as had his father. One of Archelaus's objectives was to demolish the rebel camp east of Hebron. With the help of Roman forces from the garrison in Syria, he mounted a massive onslaught which the patriots could not withstand .

In the midst of the violent clash, Judah ben Hezekiah caught sight of Shira a dozen paces to his right. Still mounted, she wielded her sword with fierce slashes, but had difficulty staying aboard the gray. Judah raced to her aid, but was felled by a blow to the back of his head.

Shira tumbled off Romulo's horse, scrambled to her feet, stumbled, and fell to the ground. A Roman soldier rolled off his horse, and checked her with the point of his sword at her throat. Struggling to avoid the blade, Shira lost her hood, exposing her face, sending her hair cascading to her waist.

The Roman was shocked at the sight of her. "What! A woman?" He gave her midriff a gentle nudge with the sword. "There you, Dominius," he hailed a comrade. "Look what we have here!"

PART TWO

CHAPTER 18

Thirty years later

With no way to measure time, Shira did not know for how long she had been shut away in her musty catacombs cell. Still quite vivid, however, were recollections of Romulo's death, the battle at Hebron where she was captured by the Romans, and the mock trial that pronounced her guilty of insurrection. And time would run out before she would forget the horrible day when Jabal was taken from her.

Her only contact with the world beyond the cell was an iron grating overhead where slender fingers of sunlight sifted through. Endless hours she spent contemplating the dusty, shimmering sun rays inching their way across the dirt floor.

Pungent odors of human waste encouraged exploration by rats and roaches which, over time, had become attentive to the sound of Shira's voice. The roaches would pause, stiffening their spindly legs, as if trying to understand what she was saying. The rats cocked their beady-eyed heads, keeping their distance. Sometimes, during the earth tremors, the rats and roaches would scamper out of sight, and Shira wished she could scamper to freedom with them. After the danger of the tremors passed, the rats and roaches returned, greeted by Shira as she might have greeted old friends.

The only sounds she heard were the voices and raucous laughter of the Roman guards filtering through the grating above. The guards often idled time away by tossing coins, and Shira listened for the victorious cackle of the one whose coin slid closest to the line drawn on the paved courtyard. Shaking her head in disgust, she heard them boast of their bawdy escapades of the night before.

Cool seasonal rains sent her hovering in a corner of the cave where she watched rivulets of water trickle across the floor, forming small streams in the dust. The rats drank from the streams, but the roaches avoided them. For a rare cleansing of her body, Shira dipped the hem of her tattered robe in the rainwater.

In the first days of her imprisonment she called up to inquire of the guards what day it was, what date, or the time of day. They responded that she was not going any place, so why did it matter? Over time she came to accept that finality, resigned to the fact that time in the dungeon really did not matter, waiting for death, with no hope of escape.

One of the older guards she dubbed "the thin one" because he appeared to have little flesh on his bones. He was kind to her, and sometimes dropped a portion of his bread to her through the grating. She heard him issue stern admonitions to his young comrades against trying to "have some of her," as they had with other women prisoners. As the years passed, she recalled hearing the thin one reprimand them for referring to her as "the old witch." Times when it was his turn to slide water and gruel under her door, she cherished the moment, for he often paused to visit, sharing bits of news of what was happening in Judea. Then, one day she didn't hear the voice of the thin one, saddened that she saw him no more.

Following her capture, Shira had tried to prepare herself for execution, since the penalty for waging war against the empire was death. Though her trial had been a forum for mockery and insult, she was incredulous that long ago death had not taken her. Why she escaped the cross or the stoning pit she had no answer. Growing up she had heard her father relate stories of prisoners who had been ignored or forgotten for years, many of them dying in the dungeons. Perhaps, she thought, she was one of those.

Weeks stretched into months, and months into years. With no way to calculate time, she did not know how many. In the early times of her imprisonment her spirit remained unbroken, and she vowed never to relinquish her convictions regarding the detested Romans. Over the years, however, she felt the weakening of her strength to resist, concerned more about staying alive than voicing protests. Pondering when her life might end, she heard the frantic cries of prisoners being dragged away who were never seen again. Emaciated by hunger and cold, she wondered why death had not come to her already.

Battling the pangs of hunger, she forced herself to down the swill and dry bread slid under her door once a day. When deepening night shadows brought chills from which there was no escape, she curled up in a corner of her cell, seeking warmth that was not there. Nights were shattered by agonized pleas for mercy. Groveling, weeping prisoners were hauled from their straw pallets by the prison guards for punishment or death. Often she heard the swish of a lash lacerating bare flesh, weeping at the outcries of the miserable victim, terrified by the frightening crunch of the Romans' ironclad boots. The next time she heard them trampling, would it end at her door?

Over time her fear dissipated to a point at which she would have welcomed the death she believed inevitable. Perhaps this, she pondered, peering about at the ugly cell, this hell hole, where rats slash the darkness with their red-eyed torches, where hunger gnaws at the insides in the middle of sleepless nights, where loneliness and isolation erode the mind– Perhaps this was the visitation of the death that she had thought certain.

In the midst of the suffering, the hunger, and the wailing voices shattering the midnight darkness, Shira contracted what she had heard called an issue of blood. Thankfully the pain was not constant.

Her hands and arms had been reduced to hardly more than skin and bones. The once flowing beauty of her hair was now stringy and gray. Only her stiffening limbs, and the creases she felt in her aging face, told her of the passing years.

From time to time strange voices drifted through the grating, as new guards replaced the old–the old, like the thin one, who had been so kind to her. One time she heard the Roman guards mention their "holiday," commemorating the death of Augustus Caesar, calling to mind her stormy encounter with the stone-faced monarch. At other times she heard references to a "procurator," a man named Pontius Pilate. Shira had no notion of his significance, but would later learn that Rome had appointed Pilate governor of Judea.

In the stillness of a mid-afternoon, when most prisoners sought refuge in sleep, the silence of the dungeon was shattered by the clamor of angry voices and rattling swords. Once, Roman guards shoved a thin-legged man with leathery skin into a cell next to hers.

"When the Baptist hears of this," the captive bawled at them, "you will suffer! The Baptist tells of him who will destroy your kind and establish his kingdom, then you will die a horrible death!"

The guards beat him, leaving him in a crumpled heap in the stench of his cell. A short time later they returned, laid hold of the bedraggled prisoner, and dragged him screaming from the cell. Shira never saw him again.

Hardly had the guards disappeared with their struggling prisoner to a chorus of jeers from other captives when Shira felt beneath her feet an eerie trembling. She had felt it before, for such quakes were common in Judea.

The rats and roaches ran for cover. The tremor lasted only a few seconds, but it shook the cave walls, crumbling cell doors, releasing the frenzied, shouting prisoners. Some wept in hysterical disbelief that the quake had set them free. Others prostrated themselves on the ground, mumbling unintelligible murmurs. All were garbed in tattered, smelly rags that scarcely covered their emaciated bodies.

Thinking only of escaping, the weak, malnourished, hollow-eyed captives were oblivious to the absence of guards who fled the courtyard seeking safety from the quake. The prisoners hurried away in all directions, losing themselves among the throngs of people flooding the streets.

Shira, caught up in the avalanche of frenetic humanity, was bewildered and felt totally alone. She shaded her eyes against the glaring sun, and cautiously ventured into the street, jostled by passersby who had taken in stride the earth movement. Swept along by the flow of foot traffic, she was confused by the clamor, and the shouts of vendors hawking their wares.

She made her way warily in the direction of the Dung gate that opened to the Bethlehem road. To be sure, she inquired of a dark, heavy-bodied man as to her whereabouts, but, startled by his gruff manner, she fled before he could answer.

Urging her weak limbs to move faster, she found herself in the midst of the swirling activity of the market place in the Lower City. The twisted streets were a mass of confusion, as she remembered them, lined with artisans' booths covered with sackcloth stretched over poles, some shaded with dry palm leaves. She wound her way past the dryers, weavers, tailors with pins stuck in their clothing. Bustling though it was, Shira discovered that once familiar places had changed but little during her years in captivity.

Priests and scribes still brandished their goose-feather quills, peddling scrolls of parchment bearing bits of their pious wisdom. She had despised their arrogance before, but now she welcomed the sight of the supercilious priests as a link to her past.

Alms seekers held out to her their palsied hands, but for them she could offer only pity.

Colliding with a tax collector displaying the badge of his profession brought to mind the image of Jeremaus, the publican. How long had it been since the time she sought from Jeremaus information regarding Roman troop movements in Judea which she would have passed to Romulo.

"Why should I risk the pain of crucifixion," the wily tax collector had said, "to aid the rebels whose cause is lost already?"

"Because you want something from me too!" she spat.

"From other women I can get the same. The streets are full of harlots who–"

"I am not a harlot!"

"–can be bought for less than I am willing to pay you."

"Then go to them," she spat, "if you don't care how many times you use a wineskin!"

"Why, you little–"

"Get out of my home, you blood sucking swine!"

Even the recollection of that unpleasant incident roused in her no anger, for she now realized that time and confinement had not robbed her of all ties to her previous life.

In her captivity, loneliness had been relieved at times by recollections of Ezlon, and of Jabal's tiny, searching fingers grasping hers, constantly exploring, never still. She played memory games of her dear friend Hannah, and Hannah's niece Miriam who married the sandal maker and sometimes invited Shira for a visit. Lamenting her l\brief times with Romulo, her thoughts of him often pushed others aside. Romulo, who begged her forgiveness, with whom she suffered in his last days.

Along the street she shrank from the reptiles poking their hideous heads above the baskets of their handlers. Soothsayers beckoned and were ignored. Entreated by elixir and magic potion peddlers to purchase their wares, all were waved aside. Mingling with the red-capped Romans, Greeks in short tunics, and bespangled women enticing men to their beds were the common people of Jerusalem. Roman guards rushed to seize him for his audacity

Caught up in the clamor, Shira huddled in the niche of a white-washed arcade, as she had sought warmth in a corner of her cell. To conceal herself from the probing eyes of curious strangers, she covered her face with her hands, and wept.

Startled by the sound of her own voice, she suddenly began to pray: "Hear, O Israel, the Lord our God, the Lord is One. Blessed be His kingdom forever and ever–" The words tumbled over themselves as though having waited for a chance to escape. In the days of her early confinement she often recited the Shema, comforted by its promise. With the prayer, revered since childhood, she felt a surge of strength flow through her body.

She dried her tear-stained face on the sleeve of her tattered robe, and bravely stepped out to continue her journey. She found the Dung gate, and struck out on the road to Bethlehem.

On the road leading south from Jerusalem, Shira recalled that it had always been heavily traveled, but seemed exceptionally crowded on this day. All about her were itinerants eager to reach the shelter of the caravansary on the outskirts of Bethlehem before nightfall. Pilgrims trudged up the rocky pathway to worship in the temple at Jerusalem, and laborers bearing axes, picks, and awls were making their way home for the night.

Shira held her breath against the stench of sweaty camels and donkeys whose handlers prodded them toward the market place. As she drew near the gate to Bethlehem, her heart leaped in anticipation. Though she could not know what awaited her there, she was happy to be home!

CHAPTER 19

In Judea it was not the best of times.

Herod's quest for absolute authority had led to death or imprisonment for anyone deemed a threat to his power. Jewish leaders, after Herod's death, had urged his son Archelaus to release thousands of political prisoners incarcerated during his father's thirty-seven year reign as king.

Archelaus had agreed to do so, then reneged on his promise, emulating his father's tyrannical rule.

Even as a youth, Herod's compulsion to dominate had been recognized by his father Antipater. Appointed by Rome as the administrator of Galilee, Antipater had bestowed upon his twenty-year-old son the governorship of Galilee. Herod was still quite young when, with the help of the emperor's troops in the year 37, he drove Antigonous from Jerusalem and, with the blessing of Rome, proclaimed himself king of Judea.

Though respected by Rome as an able ruler, Herod was despised by the people he ruled. They abhorred his pseudo generosity, charging that "the container was poisoned at the source."

Caesar himself, learning of Herod's execution of his own sons, had been heard to say, "It is better to be Herod's dog than his son."

And so it was, upon his death, that Herod passed to his son Archelaus the torch of terror. Mounting opposition to his bloody reign only encouraged Archelaus to slaughter more prisoners than he set free. In the tenth year of his reign, a delegation of religious authorities was dispatched to Rome to plead with Augustus Caesar to recall Archelaus. Caesar obliged, and Archelaus was banished to Gaul where he later died.

Caesar's death in the year14 placed Roman authority in the hands of his adopted son, Tiberius. A man of dubious integrity, Tiberius curtailed the religious rites of all foreigners in Rome, specifically those of Jewish heritage, stripped them of ritual vestments, enslaving any who defied his edict.

Hardly less palatable were conditions in Judea. Reduced by Tiberius to the status of a province, Judea was immediately subjected to stringent Roman law. Tiberius further inflamed the incensed Jews by transferring the seat of government from Jerusalem, where it was established by King David a thousand years before, to Caesarea, one of the late Herod's many tributes to the Roman emperor. Exacerbating the wrath of the Jews even further, Tiberius appointed Pontius Pilate to the position of Procurator of Judea.

With little regard for the welfare of the Jewish people, it was common practice for Rome appointed governors to bloat their pockets with taxes and assessments. So it was with Pilate. A man of little substance, and less compassion for those he ruled, Pilate's goal was to collect as much tribute as possible, as rapidly as possible, and return with his riches to the Eternal City to live out his life in luxury.

With the avarice of a hungry wolf, Pilate's tyranny proved second only to that of Herod.

Not content to govern and collect taxes, Pilate infuriated the Judeans by displaying images of Caesar in public places, in defiance of Jewish law. He also raided the temple coffers, and settled with the sword matters that civil authorities could have resolved without bloodshed.

Pilate's tyranny manifested itself one recent day when a group of merchants gathered near the governor's palace to protest his latest tax increase. Pilate, who had condescended to grant them an audience, faced them with contempt.

"Go back to your shops and forges," he scowled. "Your rights are whatever I say they are!"

"But, how can we live if so much of what we earn is paid in taxes?" they protested. "We must buy raw materials and feed our families."

"Call upon your God, you whiners! You say he is almighty. He is most high! Well, if this disturbance continues, I will show you who is most high!"

The crowd gave way as a tent maker named Levi stepped to the front of the group. Tall and sturdy of body, his sharp eyes bored into the face of the insensitive Pilate. In a calm voice, Levi said to the procurator, "You are sucking the lifeblood from the people of Judea."

Roman guards rushed to seize him for his audacity, but Pilate stopped them with the wave of a hand. "Let him speak," Pilate smirked. "The sooner they have their say, the sooner they will get back to work."

"You have mocked our God," said Levi. "Caesar himself granted us the freedom to worship. But, you have desecrated our temple, and blasphemed our God with your graven images. Even Herod–"

"Silence him!" Pilate screamed, and the guards swept down on the defenseless tradesmen, slaughtering every one.

***

Surely it had been by some providential manifestation that Jochai the sandal maker had not been among the protesters on that day. All Bethlehem knew that Jochai was as strongly opposed to the Romans' unfair taxes as any of his fellow tradesmen. And, had his wife Miriam not called him to retrieve their youngest son from a fall into the cistern, Jochai certainly would have been in the front ranks of the protest, run through by the sword of a Roman guard.

Shuddering at the thought, Jochai looked up from the sandal he was cobbling and saw a tall, beardless man, standing rigid as a pole, smiling at him. The man had appeared without notice, holding out to him a leather thong the length of a foot for which he wanted Jochai to make a pair of sandals.

"They must be this long," said the man, stretching the thong along the cobbler's bench. Beside that thong he placed a shorter one. "And this wide."

Jochai had never seen a foot of such great size. With a skeptical eye he appraised the man who awaited his response. The man appeared to be of sound mind, wearing a fine robe with a plaited sash. His sandals, Jochai noticed, were not fancy but well built. With a deep sigh, Jochai gave his balding head a dubious shake.

For Jochai it had not been a good day. Early spring rains brought with them unusually cool weather, and he awoke that morning with a cold that stuffed his massive chest. Six feet tall, he weighed a robust two-hundred-twenty-seven pounds, and in his forty-nine years he had almost never suffered a cold, nor even a sniffle. Proud he was of his freedom to eat and drink whatever Miriam put on the table. His physician had told him he was healthy as a he-goat. Ephraim should know, for he had cared for Jochai's family since he delivered the first of his seven children.

So, a cold in the chest or any other place was a rare annoyance for the sandal maker. Yet, there he was, and had been all day, sniffling and coughing and blowing his nose. Then, adding to his discomfort, there was Rabbi Eleazar, who always bargained for the lowest price for a pair of sandals, leaving little margin for profit.

"This is something you can do," the rabbi was wont to say with unsettling piety,

And he was right, Jochai conceded. He was a good sandal maker, a true craftsman, proud of his profession, as his father and grandfather had been. People came from as far away as Jericho, Hebron, and Bethany to his little shop in Bethlehem, knowing they would get quality workmanship at a reasonable price. Even so, "something you can do" was how he earned a living, fed his wife and kids, and kept a roof over their heads. If he had made sandals for every priest and rabbi in the village at Eleazar's price, his family would have long since starved.

Adding to Jochai's annoyance was Miriam's Aunt Hannah who lay ill in Capernaum, where she had gone to be with her cousin Simon a year ago and had not returned. Miriam was Hannah's favorite relative and, with no children of her own, she doted on her niece. When Jochai and Miriam were first married nearly thirty years ago, Hannah sometimes invited Miriam for a visit along with Hannah's friend Shira.

Jochai had not thought of Shira for years, but he now wondered briefly what had become of her. The last time he knew, Shira was involved in some kind of political situation, but he could not remember whether that was before or after Herod died. Miriam could not go to Capernaum to see after Hannah. She had enough to keep her busy at home, caring for the children, keeping the house in order. Responsibility of seeing after Hannah, therefore, fell upon the broad shoulders of the head of the family. Jochai did not look forward with pleasure to the journey north to cope with the problem that answered to the name of Aunt Hannah. Would it be best to bring her back to Bethlehem, which she never should have left in the first place? Or should he arrange for her care, leaving Hannah with her kinsman Simon in Capernaum? Aunt Hannah was a burden he could easily have done without, but about which he must do something.

And now here was this stranger, asking him to make a pair of sandals as long as a plow share. A glance at the man's feet told Jochai they would be swallowed up by the sandals he ordered.

"How soon do you need your sandals?" Jochai said.

"Oh," said the man, "they're not for me."

The sandal maker was having difficulty maintaining his patience. Most people ordered their own sandals. He had heard that even the High Priest, Caiaphas, went personally to the cobbler's to be measured for sandals.

"The sandals that you want me to make are not for yourself?" Jochai said.

"No, sir."

"Then, would you be good enough to tell me, sir, for whom I am to cobble a pair of sandals the likes of which Goliath might have worn to lead the Philistines against King Saul?"

The man smiled."You haven't heard?" said he.

Jochai shook his gray-fringed head, knowing not what he had not heard. "No," said he, "I haven't heard."

"You haven't heard of the voice crying in the wilderness? The sandals are for John."

"John–"

"The Baptist. John the Baptist!"

Jochai stared in disbelief.

From the hills of Judea had come a big, bearded man, clad in goatskin named Jochanan who presented himself as the forerunner of the messiah. Known to his followers as John the Baptist, much of his time was spent in the waters if the Jordan River where he baptized converts to "the ways of the Lord."

Jochai had heard of the Baptist. He also had heard some people claim that John was the messiah. Others called him "a self-serving itinerant preacher.' Never having seen the Baptist nor heard his preachments, however, Jochai was not inclined to voice an opinion regarding the wandering evangelist, but some people he knew he knew had. John's avid followers were not willing to accept that he was only who he said he was: the standard bearer for "Him Who is yet to come." Some said he was the prophet Elijah returned to life, which John vehemently denied.

With a strong look into the face of the man awaiting his response, Jochai promised to have John's sandals ready in three days. He had them done in two.

Explaining to Miriam that he had to go to Capernaum to see what needed to be done about Aunt Hannah, he may as well deliver the Baptist's sandals on the way. Oh, yes, he knew it would be a difficult journey over the hills and valleys to Capernaum. Even so, a vigorous, robust man like himself, eager as he was to observe first hand the Baptist of whom he had heard so much, could make the trip along the Jericho road to the banks of the Jordan without incident. Yes, he agreed with Miriam, he probably should not be gone so long from his cobbling, but he was confident that his eldest son David and the other boys could take care of it until he returned.

Accepting with some misgiving her husband's intentions, Miriam nonetheless packed a pouch with fresh barley bread, goat cheese, dates, and a full wineskin, food enough to sustain him until he reached Capernaum if he was frugal.

Jochai slung the pouch and a bedroll over his shoulder, assured his wife and children that he would be careful along the way, and that he most certainly would convey to Aunt

Hannah their love and good wishes. So saying, the sandal maker set off on his journey, with a giant sized pair of sandals tucked inside the bedroll.

CHAPTER 20

Hardly more than an hour's journey south of Jerusalem the village of Bethlehem clung to the mountainside, a cluster of square mud-and-straw houses whose yellow roofs shone in the late afternoon sun. Bethlehem was a bustling crossroads for caravans on their way to the markets of Egypt and Jerusalem. The caravansary, established a thousand years before in the time of King David, still accommodated weary wayfarers in the birthplace of the shepherd king.

Near Bethlehem lay the tomb of Rachel, the wife for whose hand Jacob had labored for fourteen years. There also was the tomb of Ruth the Moabite who, after the death of her husband, sojourned with her mother-in-law Naomi to Bethlehem. In the field below the village, Boaz had discovered Ruth gleaning behind the reapers, and "took her unto himself."

Approaching the village where she was born, married Ezlon, and gave birth to her son Jabal, Shira recalled the birth of the babe in Bethlehem who some believed to be the messiah, prompting Herod's maniacal fear of losing his throne to a mere babe. A bitter memory.

Spike-helmeted Roman soldiers lounged near the village gate, rekindling in Shira the fires of hatred. She swept past them with tacit defiance. In the market place she felt upon her the gawking eyes of wealthy Jews from Damascus, Antioch, and Alexandria. Milling about were craftsmen, shopkeepers, merchants who elbowed their way through the crowd to hawk their wares, and officials parading their arrogant presence.

From the village well the women of Bethlehem strode toward home, balancing on their heads earthen ware pitchers filled with water. Shira's heartbeat quickened at sight of a woman she thought to be her friend Hannah. "Are you Hannah?" Shira said.

"Hannah? No," the woman said. "I am Deborah."

"Please, forgive me, I am–"

"You're looking for Hannah?"

"Yes," Shira said, "an old friend who lived on this street."

"Oh," the woman said, "there was a woman named Hannah. I don't know if she's still there. I can tell you where she was the last I knew."

The woman directed her to where she thought Hannah might be found. Excited at the prospect of seeing her friend again, Shira wound her way through the narrow streets. Candles flickered from windows in the gathering dusk, and the tantalizing aroma of cooking food escaped open doorways.

She paused in front of a small house she remembered as Hannah's from years ago. The woman at the well had said, "That's where Hannah once lived." Shira was suddenly struck with apprehension that Hannah, after all those years, may no longer live there. Catching sight of the mezuzah mounted on the door post, she pondered how long it had been since she last saw the decorative pouch containing the five books of Moses. For that she had no answer. A faint smile crept across her pallid lips as she caressed with her fingertips the cherished symbol of God's assurance for his chosen people.

Receiving no response to her rap on the door, almost she turned away, then suddenly the door flew open, and a stocky, heavy-browed young man glared at her.

"What is it you want?" he demanded.

Shira was so startled that she could hardly speak. "Well, I– I–only–"

"Speak up, old woman! What are you doing here?"

Shira wanted to flee, but her feet would not move.

"Hannah," she said, wishing she had not come, wanting only to get away. "I– My friend Hannah–"

"Hannah?" His manner softened. "Hannah doesn't live here anymore. The last we knew, she had gone to Capernaum to be with a kinsman."

"Oh, I–"

"Are you all right?"

"All– Yes, I'm– No, please–" She collapsed at his feet.

The man called to someone inside the home, and a moment later beside him appeared a dark haired young woman."What is it, Jason?" she said his wife Rachel. He eyes then fell upon the fallen Shira. Rushing to her side, Rachel said, "Come, Jason, help me get her inside."

***

Jochai soon learned that he was not the only person who journeyed to the Jordan that day. Surrounded by wayfarers, he wondered if they too were off to see the Baptist. All about him were families, some with small children in carrying baskets, some mounted on donkeys. There, also, were litters bearing the lame and infirm. Others hobbled along on crude crutches, or assisted by loved ones, all determined to somehow bask in the presence of the prophet, who they heard could heal infirmities.

Curiosity seekers also spilled over the narrow roadway. Even white-robed priests strode briskly by with decorative phylacteries dangling from their waist bands. Jochai pondered why the priests would undertake such an arduous journey, since they rarely ventured that far afield.

With his cobbler's practiced eye he instinctively observed the various types of footwear worn by fellow travelers. Like most experienced cobblers, he could determine a man's social status by the quality of the sandals he wore.

The man had told him that the sandals tucked inside his bedroll were for John the Baptist. Jochai had heard that the Baptist was "a giant of a man," bigger than anyone he had ever seen. But did the man really live whose feet were big enough to fill the sandals he had made for the prophet? He would soon know.

Laughter and light chatter abounded among the playful younger pilgrims, while in the faces of the older ones, Jochai read solemnity and uncertainty of what they might find at the end of their journey.

Filling the air were heated condemnations of Pilate's recent massacre of the tradesmen, and idle comments about the earth movement that had rippled through Jerusalem with little more than passing notice. Mostly, though, the talk was of the rough-hewn prophet who baptized converts in the River Jordan.

"This John the Baptist fellow," Jochai heard a man say. "Is that where you're going?"

His sallow-faced neighbor complained, "It looks like the whole world is going there today."

"What do you make of him?"

"Hah!" the other scoffed. "A total impostor! Total, total impostor! A charlatan who seeks only fame and fortune for himself."

The first man, tall and slender, carriage erect, eyes keen and clear, cast him a dubious look. "A charlatan?" he said.

"A bona fide phony if there ever was one," the other sneered. "Claiming to be the messiah, indeed!"

"I hadn't heard that he claimed to be the messiah."

"Well, he may not have said it, but he's got everybody believing it. He has said everything, except to declare himself the Promised One!"

"If you feel that way, why are you going to see him?"

"I want to be there when they to see it when it happens. Look around you. Caiaphas has sent his people to interrogate this John fellow and expose him for who he really is. If he tells them he is the messiah–hah-ho! Hah-hah-ho!"

"Even if he doesn't claim to be the messiah, I'll wager Caiaphas will find an excuse to berate him. The high priest loathes anyone who draws a bigger crowd than himself."

"We'll see," the sallow-faced one chortled. "Mark my word–we will see!"

Jochai heard no more, but what he heard, and who said it, he would later recall.

The snows of Mount Gilboa had not begun their slide down to the Jordan. The slopes were teeming with beech, fig, and sycamore trees. A leopard, wary of increasing numbers of travelers, hid himself in the heavy foliage, stalking its prey along the river.

Waist deep in the waters of the Jordan, the Baptist waited patiently for the pilgrims who settled near the river's edge. Some spread blankets, while others erected thatch-roofed shelters, prepared for an extended stay. All had come to absorb the prophecies of the goatskin-clad preacher with the frowzy beard and booming voice.

With long, hairy arms wide spread, John welcomed them, inviting one and all to come closer, not as a magician might entice the crowd, nor as a thespian seeks the applause of his audience, but as one who had something of great significance to share with those who came.

"Come!" John entreated with a strong voice. "Come closer! Hear the word of the Lord, and repent of your sins!"

The Baptist exuded vitality, and confidence that he had been commissioned to prepare the world for its king.

As the company of pilgrims swept down to the Jordan from the Jericho road, Jochai was astonished at the throng of people already there. He worked his way through the mob, seeking a better view of the man who urged them to come into the water and "wash away your sins! Coming is one who is greater than I, for he existed long before me," John extolled. His dark, deep set eyes flashing with the fire of his message. "Before anything else was, he was with God. He has forever been alive, and is himself God! All that is, he created, and nothing exists, except by his hand!"

To Jochai's left, white-robed temple priests were observing closely the Baptist's behavior. One of them stepped forward and called to John where the Baptist stood in the water."Are you the messiah?" said the priest, loudly enough for all to hear.

"I am not the messiah, priest," John said with strained patience, for he had been so questioned many times before. "Nor am I worthy to be his slave!"

"If you are not the messiah," the priest said with a haughty air, glancing about, seeking his peers' approval, "then who are you?"

"Such baseless questions serve only to degrade him whose sandals I am not worthy to latch."

His denials only enhanced the suspicions of the temple delegation."Tell us, then," the priest persisted. "Are you the resurrected prophet Elijah?"

"I am not the messiah, and I am not the prophet Elijah."

"What then have you to say for yourself? We must return with the answer to those who sent us."

The Baptist drew himself up to his six-foot-six height, his piercing eyes shooting through those who would berate him. "I am a voice crying in the wilderness," he roared, "as Isaiah forewarned. Get ready for the coming of the Lord!"

His inquisitors fell away, covering their faces with their arms, as if struck by the fire of John's words.

"I baptize with water," John shouted, "but he who comes after me baptizes with the Holy Spirit!"

Turning quickly away, the priests questioned him no more. If Caiaphas's plot had been to discredit the Baptist, his agents would bring him no pleasant news.

John watched them go. "You brood of vipers!" he shouted to their departing backs. You try to escape the fires of hell without turning to God! That is your reason for being cleansed through baptism. First you must go and prove that you are worthy, that you have repented of your sins, by the way you treat your fellowman. Because you are sons of Abraham, do not think you are safe! From the stones of the desert God can create sons of Abraham!"

His listeners quaked as he admonished them to be baptized, "to show that you have turned to God, and away from your wicked ways, in order to be forgiven for your sins. Come unto me and be cleansed in the name of him whose coming you await!"

Many were persuaded, moving from their places on the river bank toward the prophet in the water. The Baptist welcomed them with open arms.

To Jochai's surprise, the first one to stumble into the water, as if he could not wait to reach the Baptist, was the sallow-faced man from the trail who had condemned the Baptist as "a total impostor!" John lifted the man from where he fell in the water, blessing him "in the name of him who comes after me."

Along the river bank the line of converts stretched without end, and the ritual of baptism by the tireless Baptist continued for hours. John took a deep breath, and stroked his brow, his eyes falling inexplicably upon a young man in the crowd whose gaze was fixed on the prophet.

Jochai followed the Baptist's gaze to the man only a few steps to his left. With shoulder length hair and a light beard, he was staring back at John. A faint smile played at the corners of his thin lips. Jochai thought he was not so different from the others, except for his eyes. Such soft, caring eyes Jochai had never seen, filled with kindness and compassion.

For a long moment the young man did not move, but kept looking at the Baptist, who seemed transfixed by his stare. He then took a step toward John, and some who had waited for hours to be blessed by the Baptist moved aside to let him pass. John watched him wade into the water, then reached out and clasped his hand.

Jochai saw John's lips move but could not hear his words. John waded with him into deeper water, where he immersed the man in the ritual of baptism. At that moment a strange and shocking thing happened. From somewhere appeared a snow white dove that lit on the shoulder of the young man John had just baptized. A wave of apprehension fell over the crowd as a great loud voice of someone they could not see declared, "This is my son in whom I am well pleased."

The young man came up out of the river, and wiped the water from his face. He then wound his way through the silent masses and up an incline, looking neither right nor left.

"Behold the lamb of God!" John's voice boomed, "the one who takes away the sins of the world!"

"It's Jesus," said a whispered voice from somewhere in the crowd. "Jesus of Nazareth!"

All eyes then followed the man called Jesus as he strode unhurriedly toward the desert wilderness.

Jochai marveled at the moment. Almost he was drawn to follow Jesus into the hills, but did not. Nor did anyone else. With the hushed crowd Jochai watched in awe as Jesus walked alone into the desert.

Turning away, Jochai came face-to-face with the man who had ordered the sandals for John the Baptist.

"I have them with me," Jochai said, removing the sandals from his bedroll.

"What is the charge?" said the other.

Jochai took a long look at the Baptist soaked to his waist in the Jordan River, tireless, unflagging, as the procession of converts seemed never to end.

"No charge," said Jochai. "That's something I can do."

Shading his eyes against the late afternoon sun, Jochai resumed his trek north to Capernaum.

CHAPTER 21

For three days Shira lay half conscious. Rachel worried herself into a frenzy, fretting over her. Rachel bathed Shira, washed and trimmed her matted hair, and replaced her tattered clothing with some of her own, doing whatever she thought would ease her discomfort.

Like most Judean women, Rachel's dark haired beauty was surpassed only by the depth of her compassionate nature. She kept a close eye on Shira, explaining to her husband Jason that she needed to stay close in case there was a sudden change in the condition of their guest. Jason responded with an indifferent shrug and went on his way.

Rachel's vigil was filled with bathing the patient with hot cloths, reducing the fever with cold cloths day and night. She spooned hot lentil soup, fresh goat's milk, and other food and liquid she thought would help restore Shira's strength. Rachel suffered with her, sharing her anguish as she writhed uncontrollably at times, crying out in delirium. "Will we never be rid of them!" At other times Shira would plead, "My baby, my baby! Please don't take my baby!"

On the fourth day the fever began to subside. Rachel went for a basin of fresh water. Returning to Shira's side, she found her eyes wide open, staring at her with a wan smile. Rachel's joy was boundless."Aha!" said she. "You've come back to us!"

Shira was grateful to Rachel for her kindness and considerate care. She told her so, and more. She talked, and Rachel listened, learning of Ezlon, and of the devastating loss of her son Jabal. She learned of Shira's childhood, her parents, and of her imprisonment. Shira told her about everything, except Romulo. Him she kept locked away in a secret compartment, opening the door only at private times when her recollections would not be disturbed.

With the aid of nourishing food and Rachel's caring hands, color began its return to Shira's cheeks, showing signs of her growing strength. Shira allowed Rachel to fuss over her for ten days more, after which Rachel pronounced her well enough to venture from the house.

On her first day out, Shira went in search of her old home, and found it occupied by an aged, stooped woman with sharp eyes, a pointed chin with little gray whiskers sticking out, and a toothless grin.

The house had changed but little since she last saw it. Its humble furnishings included the bushel, grain mill, the weaving frame, and the serving table. Through the narrow doorway she saw the bed of straw in the adjoining room—the room from which Romulo had escaped the despicable search of Major Cassio—and the bed upon which Romulo awakened emotions she had thought long dead. How long ago? She could not say, but the hint of a remembering smile touched her lips.

The woman poured wine and asked Shira why she had come.

"I've been away for many years," Shira said, "but my son and I once lived in this house—after his father was killed."

"Oh, it's so painful, losing a loved one," said the woman. "Are you back in Bethlehem to stay?"

"No. Not yet any way. I'll be leaving soon for a visit with a friend in Capernaum."

When she said goodbye, the kind lady squeezed her hand and wished her well. Shira's next outing took her to the pottery shop where she spent many hours of her childhood watching her father mold bowls and urns from globs of clay.

"Shira!" said Joel, the proprietor, when she told him who she was. "Shira bas Haran! Oh, how I wish my father were here to see you. He loved you so." With a chuckle, he said, "More than he loved me, I think."

"Isaac is not here?"

"My father died seven years ago." He cast her an inquisitive glance. "We were afraid you had died also, since we hadn't heard from you for so long."

"Yes. I thought you might have forgotten me."

"We never forgot. We spoke of you often, and wondered what had become of you." He turned to a desk drawer and brought out a ledger. "We never forgot you," Joel said, "and we never forgot our obligation to you." He held up the ledger for her to see. "Every year we set aside the amount we agreed on as payment. We didn't know when you might return, and we wanted to have your portion ready when you came."

"Thank you, Joel."

"Come around again in a few days and I'll have everything in order for you."

Joel had been as good as his promise. Shira was shocked at the amount that had accumulated over the years, and declared Joel's obligation satisfied.

"The shop is now yours," she said. "I hope you enjoy it as much as my father did."

***

During the evening meal, Rachel said to Shira," You're welcome to stay with us as long as you like." She cast Jason a look that told him not to object.

"You are much too kind," Shira said. "I have imposed on you for long enough.

However, when I return from Capernaum, perhaps we can talk about that. I would expect to pay you, of course,."

"Whatever is fair," Jason said. "As for your going to Capernaum, I have a friend who makes trips up that way sometimes. I might be able to arrange passage for you the next time he goes." He poked at his food. "Maybe he can help you avoid some of the unsavory characters you might run into along the way." He looked at Rachel to emphasize his point. "Especially an itinerant so-called Baptist who spends his time dunking unsuspecting people in the Jordan River."

Shira said, "Speaking of Baptists, there's something I've been wanting to ask you."

"Ask away," Jason said.

"What is it, Shira?" said Rachel.

"Who is John the Baptist?"

Her question was greeted with silence. She noted Rachel's quick glance at Jason. He concentrated on his food.

Rachel said, "John the Baptist is a man who–"

"Rachel!" Jason said.

Rachel brushed her mouth with a hand cloth, shot a reproving look at her husband, and said, "John the Baptist is a man whose name–"

"We do not speak of him in this house, Rachel," Jason said.

"–we are not permitted to utter it because my husband doesn't agree with what he preaches."

"He's a lunatic!" Jason said. "Caiaphas himself says he's a lunatic."

"The high priest is hardly the best judge of that,"

Rachel said.

"Running around over the countryside half naked," Jason went on. "Dressed in goat skin, screaming to the hills, 'Repent of your sins!' Who gave him the authority to demand the repentance of sins?"

Silence hung heavy as they dabbed at their food, until Shira said, "The day of the quake that I told you about–when the prisoners escaped–the guards dragged away a man who shouted at them, 'When John the Baptist hears about this, you will suffer.'"

Jason shifted his stocky body uneasily, not sure he wanted to hear more of what she had to say about the Baptist.

"It was soon after that," Shira said, "when the earth shook, and the cell doors fell away."

"If you're looking for some kind of omen in this, Shira," Jason said, "I'm sure it was nothing more than coincidence. Earth movements happen around here all the time. I don't see how a connection could be made between a minor tremor and some loony Baptist." He sopped a chunk of bread in gravy and crammed it in his mouth. "One day this John fellow will come to the same end as others who have claimed to be the messiah–either on the cross or in the stoning pit."

"John does not claim to be the messiah," Rachel protested. "He claims only to be the forerunner of the Expected One.""Enough, Rachel! Who but a lunatic would risk his life condemning Herod for stealing his brother's wife?"

"That's common knowledge," said Rachel. "Everybody knows Herod Antipas stole his brother's wife."

"But nobody ever said it out loud before," Jason said. "Antipas has John under guard at Tiberius, and would execute him, except he's afraid John might be Elijah back from the tomb. Antipas is as daft as John. He's scared out of his wits that he'll be punished for his father's evil."

"Antipas has evil enough of his own," Rachel reminded him, "without borrowing from the tyrant beast."

"Jochai is the only man I know," Jason said, "who puts any stock in what that Baptist fellow says. He was there when John baptized that Nazarene, proclaiming him the savior of the world. A Nazarene? Savior of the world!" he scoffed as he rose to leave.

"Jochai is not one to take such things lightly," Rachel pointed out. "You've always respected him as a man of strong beliefs."

"He's wrong on this one," Jason shot back on his way out. "Who but a lunatic would believe that anything good would come out of Nazareth?"

Once Jason was gone, Shira said to Rachel, "This Jochai that Jason mentioned–"

"The sandal maker," Rachel said. "He was a close friend of Jason's father. Jason anticipates the arrival of the messiah on a great white steed, breathing fire, brandishing a flaming sword, and taking over the world. Jochai is more practical. He believes the Messiah's purpose will be to conquer evil. Banishing the Romans is only a part of his promise."

"And Miriam?" said Shira. "Does she believe as Jochai does?"

"Miriam? You know Jochai's wife?"

"She's the niece of my friend Hannah. We were once friends."

"Of course! I remember now. I have heard Miriam speak of you. Jochai recently returned from a visit with Hannah. He says she isn't well, but chooses to stay in Capernaum with her kinsman, a fisherman named Simon."

CHAPTER 22

Shira's instructions were to join the caravan at the trade center in Jerusalem. From there the caravan would take the Jericho road up the Jordan valley, traveling north from there to Capernaum on the shore of the Sea of Galilee.

Arriving early at the caravan staging area, Shira decided to use the time to reacquaint herself with the city of Jerusalem, which she had been eager to leave behind after she escaped the dungeon. She skirted the clamor of the market place, unable to avoid the hubbub along the twisting, congested streets swarming with pilgrims, and alms seekers. Trudging through the Lower City toward the Temple, her heart leaped at sight of the towering, shimmering magnificence of the Temple rising from Mount Zion.

In the eighteenth year of his reign, Herod the Great, in a feeble attempt to appease the Jews' resentment toward him, had ordered the Temple rebuilt. Now its halls were lined with bazaars, and booths with animals and doves for sale to worshipers for sacrifices on the altar. Prominent also were the booths of the money changers, for no foreign currency was permitted inside the Temple.

At the entrance to the Hall of Polished Stone she paused, recalling her long ago appeal to the Sanhedrin for aid to the rebel forces. How different the history of Judea might have been, she lamented, had the Council lent its support to the efforts of the patriots.

Passing the Court of the Gentiles, she became aware that some intuitive thing had drawn her to the Temple in search of Rabbi Jacob, once a dear friend of her father's. Winding her way through the maze of activity she reached the Porch of Solomon where she encountered a group of white-robed students sitting in a circle, listening intently to a man she supposed was a rabbi. She could see only the back of his head, but was struck by the strangeness of his words.

"I say to you, love your enemies, do good to those who do evil to you, and bless those who curse you. If you love only those who love you," the gentle voice continued, "what credit is that to you? For even sinners have those who love them."

His hearers began to disperse, and Shira heard no more.

She was delighted to find Rabbi Jacob still able to teach in the Temple. Seated on a stone bench near the Porch of Solomon, aged and gaunt, he was dismissing a class of young disciples.

"Mine is a story that would take much time to tell," she said after she and Jacob exchanged greetings. "As I searched for you, I heard a man speaking in a way that I never heard before."

"I hope it was not as disturbing as you appear, my dear," said the old scholar.

"Only that I didn't understand the meaning of his words. He spoke of loving our enemies, and those who curse us, and– His voice was kind and gentle."

"Was his name Jesus?" said Jacob with a wan smile.

"I never heard his name, but someone called him 'master.'"

"The Nazarene."

She was reminded that Jason had mentioned a Nazarene when he criticized the Baptist.

"Jesus was born in Bethlehem," Jacob explained, "during the reign of the fist Herod, at the time of Caesar's census. Some believed that Jesus was the new-born king of the Jews. Herod, fearing the loss of his throne, decreed that all male children–"

"–two years of age and younger be put to death," Shira said.

"You remember that?"

"My son was one of them."

"Oh, my child! In my advanced age, my memory–"

"This Jesus, then," she said, "was the infant whom Herod sought to destroy?"

"Yes." Thoughtfully he stroked his yellowing beard. "Jesus is the one."

She caught a quick breath."Then it was because of him that my Jabal was taken from me?"

"Dear Shira, whatever we know of him, we cannot blame Jesus for the sins of Herod. Even your father Haran, strong willed as he was, would have agreed to that. The loss of your son would not have been the wish of Jesus."

"Do you believe it, rabbi?"

"Believe it?"

"That he is the one who will rescue us from oppression."

With a deep sigh, the ancient teacher gave his gray head a patient shake. How many times had he debated that question with both students and scholars, arriving at no satisfactory conclusion?

"Jesus is a teacher and sometimes prophet, Shira. He is denigrated by some because they–no, we–don't understand him. Some believe because they so need the assurance of him for whom we are taught to wait. Jesus bids his followers trust that one day they will be free of the bonds of sin–not necessarily the bondage of Rome. But, there is much that we don't know about Jesus." With a sad smile, he said, "With all my heart I regret the sorrow that you have been made to suffer with the loss of your son. Still, we must remember that the Lord places upon us only those burdens that we are strong enough to bear. Only He knows his purposes. Our lot is to do the bidding of Him whom we worship as our God."

"Rabbi Jacob," Shira said with a pensive nod, "do you think it strange that Jesus was the only one who escaped Herod's slaughter?"

"I know only that, according to legend, his parents fled to Egypt at the behest of an angel, and took the child with them. Then, following Herod's death, they returned with the babe to Galilee."

"Is it wrong to wish harm to someone who has harmed you?"

"Recall the words that you heard Jesus speak. Love your enemies, bless those who curse you. Vengeance is the endeavor of fools, my child. Some otherwise great men, King Saul among them, have been consumed by the fires of jealousy and revenge. You are not a fool, Shira bas Haran. In Judea there is a great need for women with your passion for living, and for justice. Use your energy to restore the pride of Judea, and God will bless you beyond measure."

"My father believed that pride is the child of freedom."

"Pride does not die with enslavement, my dear. Of all the qualities that we Jews have drawn unto ourselves, our pride of heritage no tyrant can wrest from us."

Aware that she likely would not see him again, Shira bade the grand old rabbi goodbye, pondering the wisdom of his words.

Learning the identity of the Nazarene, a disturbing

thought forced its way into Shira's consciousness. She elbowed her way through the hordes of people. Struggling with the nagging thought, she stumbled and fell to the floor of Solomon's Porch. Immediately she felt a hand touching hers, helping her to her feet. In that brief moment she caught a glimpse of the man's tanned face. Even from that brief moment, the gentleness of his eyes, and the sadness of the smile on his thin lips, she would not forget.

***

At the staging area Shira was pleased to learn that Jason's friend was Shukar, her teen aged oxcart companion from years ago on the journey from Beth-hoglah to Jerusalem.

"You are Shukar," she said, "a friend of Jason's?"

"I am," said he. "And you are Shira?"A husky, broad shouldered man with an easy manner, he peered into her face with a curious smile."Have we met before, Shira?"

"Once on an oxcart long ago I met a young man named Shukar who thought it strange that I had no wisdom to share with my friends."

With a hearty laugh he grabbed her in a strong embrace. "But I never knew your name," he said.

"Belthad thought it best that no one know."

"Ah, yes, Belthad."

Shukar escorted her to where a restless donkey scraped the dry earth with a sharp hoof.

Shira said, "A good man, I believe you said of Belthad."

"Yes. He taught me how to be a merchant, and a man." Helping her onto the back of the donkey, he said, "We'll be getting underway soon. It's a long ride to Capernaum, but we'll make you as comfortable as possible."

"Thank you, Shukar."

"You can still call me Shukie," he said with a smile.

***

Shukar kept the caravan moving at a steady pace, pausing only long enough to allow the animals occasional rest and grazing along the way–one of the many things he learned from his mentor Belthad.

Shira, weary of her seat on the swaying, sometimes balky donkey, often dismounted and walked for a while, stretching her legs, chatting with other members of the party.

At sunset Shukar gave the order for the caravan to halt. The handlers cared for the animals, then settled around small campfires. Above the fires were suspended cauldrons of soup for the evening meal, along with rounds of bread and cups of wine, accompanied by a lively exchange of stories and laughter.

Shukar spotted Shira by the fire and sat down beside her. "Earlier you mentioned Belthad," he said. "When the Romans found out he was freighting food and medical supplies to Romulo and the rebels, they crucified him."

Shira, though saddened by the news of Belthad's tragic death, could not suppress the secret smile stealing across her lips at the sound of Romulo's name. She no longer dwelt on her loss of Romulo, having long since shed her last tears for the Jew/Roman whose last word– "Shira!"– had echoed across the years, robbing her of peaceful slumber. Yet, etched on her heart of precious memories was the contentment of having been loved by the man she had tried to hate but could not.

Shukar said, "I was not on that last trip with Belthad. But, from him I learned what it means to commit oneself to a cause. Belthad hated the Romans, but he loved his country more than his own life. And he died for it, as surely as if he had been run through on the field of battle."

They fell silent, attentive to the merriment going on around them.

"Romulo was such a man," Shukar said then.

"Yes."

"Others have tried to stir the people to revolt, but to many, power was more important than freedom. The road to Jericho has been lined with the crosses of those who resisted Roman authority."

"I know nothing of this," she said. She chose the moment to tell him of her years in the dungeon, and why she was taken prisoner, isolated from the outside world.

Shukar gave his head a sad shake."You knew Romulo then?" he said. "And Judah. You knew Judah also?"

"Yes, I knew Judah."

"I have heard that Judah was blinded in the battle of Herodium and was no longer able to lead the rebels in Galilee."

Judah? Had he not died in the battle outside Herodium where she was taken prisoner?

Her last recollection of Judah was of his trying to reach her, being felled by a blow from a Roman lance.

"Shukie," she said, puzzled at his account of what happened to Judah, "are you saying that Judah ben Hezekiah is alive?"

"Somewhere. Who knows where? The Romans no longer care about him. What can a blind man do that would threaten the empire?"

She gave that a moment of silent thought."Is Jason one of those who might threaten the empire?" she said.

"Jason is a dedicated anarchist," he said. "He hates Rome, he hates the Pharisees, he hates Pontius Pilate. Jason is a good friend, but he and I are worlds apart in our political thinking. Jason hates anything that smacks of authority."

"That must include itinerant evangelists."

"I wouldn't be surprised. Why do you say that?"

"We had a discussion about a man named John the Baptist. Jason says he is a lunatic."

"You noticed the droves of people we passed along the road from Jericho?"

"Yes. I wondered who they were, and where they were going."

"They probably were on their way to see the Baptist who holds forth along the Jordan. He claims to be the forerunner of the messiah."

"And all those people were his followers?"

"They don't know if he is who he claims to be, but from what I've heard, he preaches a very strong message. Repent of your sins, for the day of judgment is at hand. Those people are

eager for someone they can believe in, and he is the nearest one to the messiah that they have heard of."

"What about the Nazarene? Jason scoffed at the notion that he could be the savior of the world."

"Nobody knows. Least of all Jason. Nothing new can enter a closed mind. Until Jason witnesses the arrival of the messiah in the manner that he envisions, everyone else is a charlatan. Aside from that, Jason is a fine man. A fine, hard headed man."

"I love his wife," Shira said.

"So do I"

Shira's attention was drawn to the images dancing in the fire at her feet.

Up from the Jordan valley Shukar's caravan creaked toward Capernaum on the banks of the Sea of Galilee. Along the way, clumps of reddish blue violets peeked through the fertile green soil. Hillsides, alive with young fruit in fresh Spring maturity, flourished with budding crocus, mandrake, and daffodils.

Having perched for so long on the back of the tenacious little donkey, Shira was relieved to see the towers of Capernaum vault into view. The bustling city lay but a short distance from where the icy waters of the Jordan plummeted into the Sea of Galilee, a major center of commerce whose business houses and market place bustled with people from many provinces of the Roman Empire. Haughty Jewish priests and scribes in tasseled robes held their heads high, hardly aware of the peasants who walked at their sides. Swarthy Greeks and lean Phoenicians, arrogant Romans in togas, and merchants from Damascus, Antioch, and

Alexandria–all rubbed elbows with beggars, footpads, harlots, and alms seekers.

Dotting the waters of the sea were fishing boats, manned by Galileans whose families since time began had supported themselves by "drawing the nets." In the inns and taverns along the shore, some fishermen sought refuge from the frustration of having hauled empty nets from bad waters.

One of those fishermen was a barrel chested, muscular Galilean with a deep red beard, Simon, the son of Jonas. Simon brought with him his brother Andrew, a good fisherman, but, unlike his younger brother, Andrew was a quiet man with a ready smile who, saying little that didn't need to be said. Simon, on the other hand, was known for his explosive temperament who often lashed out with little forethought.

"Hie there, you Simon!"

Simon heard the jeering voice from across the room. Obadiah was at it again.

It had not been a good day for the brothers. The fish had eluded their nets, Cousin Hannah had another attack, and the Master, against Simon's judgment, had spoken again of going up to Jerusalem for the Passover. Jesus and the twelve had gone to Jerusalem for the Holy Day observance the past two years without incident. Simon opposed the journey this time, however, because he knew the temple priests, and High Priest Caiaphas in particular, sought to discredit Jesus as a blasphemer and heretic on account of his teachings.

And now here sat the caustic Obadiah who somehow could sense when things had not gone well. For reasons known only to him, Obadiah seemed to search for ways to belittle Andrew, and for much too long had done so.

With a nod in Andrew's direction, Obadiah said, "Is that your best catch of the day, Simon?" eliciting derisive chuckles around the room.

In times past Simon had responded to Obadiah's taunts with blistering retorts, even challenging him to "settle this right here once and for all," but Obadiah had wisely backed down, averting possible destruction at the hands of the big fisherman. On this day though, Simon held his tongue, motioning Andrew to a table.

All eyes focused on Simon, whose patience with Obadiah's jabs at his brother must have been stretched to the limit. They expected him to explode at any moment, as he had in times past, and set Obadiah awash in a sea of invective.

Even so, Simon joined his brother at the table, ordered a bowl of wine for himself, and one for Andrew. When the innkeeper brought the wine, Simon thanked him profusely for his kindness, and sipped at it in total serenity, as he had learned from the Master perhaps.

Obadiah was puzzled by Simon's tranquil behavior, and looked around the room as if seeking the answer in the faces of his friends who shook their heads in disbelief. What had come over the big fisherman? In times past Simon would have left the tavern in shambles, a victim of his fiery temper. Why had he not lashed out now as they had seen him do before, allowing no one to best him in a confrontation?

Simon finished his wine and got to his feet. Andrew waited beside him. Simon wiped his wine wet lips with the back of his hand, facing his tormentor. "Obadiah,' said he, "you are a good friend. Because of that, for many years I have endured your belittling of my brother Andrew. How he got to be the butt of your barbs, snide remarks, and attempts to intimidate him

I do not know. But, they are no longer amusing. As you can see–" He placed an arm across his brother's shoulders."–my brother is unaffected by your insults, for he is a strong man who resists in silence. But, I am not so strong. One day you will go too far, and when that day comes, if he does not cut out your tongue and feed it to you, I will." He dropped a coin on the table, and headed for the door.

Obadiah and his cronies were stunned to open mouthed awe as, without another word,\ nor a backward glance, the brothers departed the premises.

***

Shira set off in search of her friend Hannah. Rachel had told her Hannah was staying at the home of a kinsman named Simon, known as the big fisherman. Half the men of Galilee could have been named Simon, but she had no difficulty in her inquiries making clear whom she was looking for. "The big fisherman" was easily distinguished from the others

Through meandering streets Shira wound her way until she found herself inspecting the front door of a modest home she believed to be that of the big fisherman. She did not know how far she had come from the market place where she promised to rejoin Shukar on his return to Jerusalem, but she was hopeful that she had found where dwelt the big fisherman.

It was a small house, neat and white-washed, much like her own in Bethlehem had been. She gave the door post a gentle rap that brought a burly man with a heavy beard.

"Are you Simon," she said, "known as the big fisherman?"

"I am Simon, yes."

"I have come to see Hannah. I was told I would find her at the home of Simon, known

as the big fisherman."

"Hannah is not well," he said with an impatient yank at his beard. "The Master is with her now. It is best that she not be disturbed."

"The Master?"

"He who has raised the dead and restored to others their sight. He is with Hannah."

"I have come all the way from Bethlehem, and I–"

"We do not question the ways of the Master," said Simon with a restless glance over his shoulder.

"Who is it, Simon?" came a woman's voice from inside the house.

Shira's heart raced. Recognizing the voice as Hannah's, she caught a quick breath.

"A woman," Simon said."A visitor to see you."

Shira said, "Tell her it is Shira. Shira bas Haran."

"She says she is Shira bas Haran."

A moment later beside Simon appeared a gray haired woman with a querulous look on her face. "You are Shira?" she said. A pleasant smile crept across her pallid lips.

"Yes, Hannah, I am Shira."

Simon stepped aside. "What of the Master?" he said.

"Oh, Simon, he has taken away the pain, as you said he would!" cried Hannah, her eyes aglow with wonder. "He said you would know where to find him."

Simon shrugged and turned away without another word.

A pleasant smile crept across Hannah's face as she took Shira in a warm embrace.

"Shira!" she said. "You're alive!"

***

In the days that followed, Shira and Hannah had much to talk about, catching up on what had happened to them since they last saw each other.

"Some of my fondest memories are of you," Hannah said, pouring the wine. "You were always so strong, so self assured. I envied you your brave manner. Were you never afraid?"

"I was afraid. Not for myself, but for Judea." Shira said. "After Jabal was taken from me, I no longer feared for myself, for I had nothing more to lose."

"Such a sad time. I tried to comfort you, but you would not be comforted."

"I wanted to destroy Herod and Caesar, and all the evil that they stood for."

"You gave people courage to resist the Romans."

"Romulo gave them the courage. I screamed a lot, but he led."

Hannah began clearing the table. "There's a new kind of revolution in Judea now," she said. "It's led by a man who believes that we should love one another. Love your neighbor, he says, and turn the other cheek when someone offends you."

Shira listened with interest. Those were the kinds of things she had heard in the Porch of Solomon, by the man Rabbi Jacob identified as the Nazarene.

"Are these the words of the one you call Master?" she said.

"Yes! He is the Master. John the Baptist himself declared him to be the messiah. The

Master healed me of unbearable pain with a touch of his hand. Oh, Shira, the ailment you told

me about– You must go to him, and hear his healing words, and feel the touch of his hand."

Listening to Hannah, Shira now believed that already she had felt the touch of his hand–in the Porch of Solomon. Even so, she was taunted yet by the dreadful notion that invaded her thoughts when Rabbi Jacob confirmed that Jesus was the babe born in Bethlehem–the one who had escaped the slaughter in which Jabal died. She tried to push the thought aside, but it would not go away.

Where was he now, this Nazarene whom Jason disparaged, whom the Baptist proclaimed as the savior of the world?

Hannah said, "Where you find Simon, you are likely to find the Master."

Not since they first met had Shira seen Simon who spent much time aboard his fishing boat, or traveling the countryside with the Master. She doubted that Simon would recognize her if they met again. But she would know him–the big fisherman with the raspy voice.

Shira refused to give in to the forces of evil at work in her mind. Assuming a light-hearted air, she said to Hannah, "A faint smile touched the corners Have I nothing better to do than to go traipsing around the country in search of a man who heals?"

"He won't be hard to find. Crowds gather wherever he speaks."

"And you think he would heal a little old Jewish lady who doesn't believe?"

"He is a prophet, Shira."

"Is Judea not overrun with prophets?"

"Please, Shira, won't you go to him? You have suffered so. Those horrible years in that dungeon–your loss of Jabal–"

The image of that tragic day never left her mind. The Romans at her door, Romulo and the two guards. Her ears rang yet with the terrified cries of her Jabal being grabbed up and whisked away.

"Hannah," she said, "do you really believe that he could make me well?"

Could she be healed by the man whose birth had been the cause of her son's death? Was she now to fall on her knees and lift up her hands and worship him? Was she to plead, "Master, forgive me for I have sinned, and make me well? And while you're at it, Master, would you please bring my son back to life?"

Hannah placed a comforting arm across her shoulders.

"Hannah," Shira sobbed. "Oh, Hannah, Hannah–"

Hannah gathered her sobbing friend in her arms, caressing her brow with gentle hands. She could only guess the true reason for Shira's distress.

***

Setting off in search of the Nazarene, Shira carried with her a demon's urgency to strike back, to avenge her loss, to harm him by whom she had been so dreadfully harmed. Rabbi Jacob had said that vengeance was the endeavor of fools. "You are not a fool," he had said. But thirty years in the dungeon had not drained the well spring of her sorrow. And now she felt as though she no longer controlled her actions, that some irresistible force had taken command of her senses.

She first looked for Jesus in the market place.

"The Nazarene?" said a man of whom she inquired. "Look for the crowd down by the seashore. He's leaving for Passover in Jerusalem."

Shira paused by a display of carving knives. She moved away. She looked back. The one with the wooden handle– No! She resisted the temptation. Cautiously she fingered the blade, reminded briefly of her encounter years before with Colonel Marius. Holding the dagger dripping with his blood, how horrified she had been. She picked up the knife, turning it over

in her hand. She wanted to put it down, trying to walk away. But something kept pulling at her. Something stronger than she. Something that seized control of her senses, as she had instinctively seized the colonel's dagger.

She lost the battle. Guessing at the value of the knife, she dropped a few coins on the table, tucked the knife inside the sleeve of her garment, and struck out down the rocky slope toward the seashore.

Hannah had told her "wherever he speaks crowds gather." Even so, Shira was amazed at the mobs of people pushing and shoving, vying for position near the Master, hoping to be healed by a look, or a touch of the hand of the young man who they had been told performed miracles.

She fought her way through the unruly throng until– There! Jesus was moving toward a small boat anchored at the shore. Hurry! She struggled until she was almost close enough to touch him. Reaching out, the press of the mob caused her to lose her footing. Stumbling headfirst, her hand touched the hem of his garment!

"Who touched me?" she heard him say.

His soft voice penetrated the din of the murmuring masses. They fell silent, and all eyes turned to the Master.

Shira lay motionless, staring into the face of the man who lifted her from the floor that day in the Porch of Solomon.

"Who touched you?" said a big man with a red beard.

The big fisherman! Stricken with fright, Shira feared that Simon might prevent her from carrying out her plan. Quickly she covered her face.

"In this huge gathering," Simon said to the Master, "how could we know who touched you?"

Jesus said, "I felt strength go out from me when someone touched me." His eyes found the distraught Shira where she had fallen at his feet.

In his eyes she saw again the compassion of the man who had rescued her in the temple. Now as then he took her hand, helping her to her knees. She felt a bolt of energy surge through her body. She tried to speak, finally finding her voice."I am the one, sir," she said. "I touched your garment."

From the crowd a caustic voice shouted, "Who is this woman?"

"Be not afraid, good woman," said Jesus. "No harm will come to you."

On the sand beside her lay the carving knife, having dropped from her sleeve when she fell. The crowd gasped.

Shira grabbed for the knife, but a man kicked it beyond her reach.

"You sought to harm me?" Jesus said.

"Only because–" She searched for words. "–because you were born, my son was murdered by the tyrant Herod."

"Your son was slain by a servant of the devil. I would not have had it so. I come, not to harm, but to heal."

Because he did not chastise her, Shira gained courage. "I have been told," she said, "that you have made the lame to walk, and that you raised a man from the grave."

"In me my father has instilled great mercy."

"My friend Hannah–" She paused with a glance at Simon. His eyes narrowed, as though trying to remember where he had seen her before. "Hannah told me that you could take away my pain caused by an issue of blood."

"Do you believe that, Shira?"

A shiver of delight rippled through her body. Of all the people pressing in around him, he had called her by name!

The impatient Simon urged Jesus toward the boat, but the concern of the Nazarene was for the woman kneeling at his feet.

"Had you turned to me before," he said to Shira, "you could have been healed already."

"I wanted to harm you," she said, "because I believed you had harmed me. I know now that you would not have wanted my son to die. And I believe you can take away my pain."

A faint smile touched the corners of his mouth. "I am not the one who heals," he said. "I only do the bidding of him who sent me." He placed a hand on her head. "Go in peace, good woman. Your faith has made you whole."

He turned away and climbed into the boat. Only briefly did he look back, his eyes resting on Shira, still kneeling on the sand. Tears streamed down her cheeks as she bowed her head and folded her hands on her lap.

She would have been distressed to know that when next she saw the Master, he would be laboring under the weight of a crude cross on which he had been condemned to die.

CHAPTER 23

On the banks of the Jordan followers of the Master were gathered around small campfires. Sitting apart from the others, a robust young man sat staring into the fire, resting his back against a boulder.

"You are Jabal?" he heard someone say.

Jabal looked up into the face of a man twice his age. "Yes," he said. "I am Jabal."

The visitor dropped to his knees beside him, folded his knees against his chest, and wrapped his arms around them. "I'm Judah," said he. "I've noticed that you seem troubled by the words of the Master."

"I'm one of the newer converts. Maybe that's why some of the things he teaches are a bit confusing."

"How did you get to know him?"

"Jesus?" Jabal said. "I was a deck hand on Simon's fishing boat. He and his brother Andrew were followers of the Master. Sometimes they would take me with them to hear him speak. At first I was skeptical. Then, one day at sea a squall blew up. I got caught in the rigging and landed on my head. When I woke up, Jesus was kneeling beside me, pressing the palm of his hand against my forehead. Simon told me later that when Jesus arrived I was dead. Needless to say, I've been following him ever since."

"In Judea," Judah said, "your name—Jabal—is not a common name."

"I never thought about it."

"I once had a friend who had a son by that name."

"Oh?"

"Would I be wrong to suggest that you and the Master are about the same age?"

"I'm thirty-three."

"And you know the Master was born in Bethlehem."

"So was I."

Judah sensed that he was on the verge of a startling discovery. But then, had Shira's son not died in Herod's massacre along with the other male children? Certainly she had believed so.

"Jabal," Judah said, "are you familiar with Herod's decree?"

"You mean when he killed the boy babies? Yes, I know about that."

"Do you think it significant that you and the Master were the only ones who survived?"

"I didn't know that. I was nine years old when my mother told me about it."

"Your mother?"

"Well, she wasn't my real mother," Jabal said with a tinge of bitterness. "Nobody knows what happened to her. She was off fighting some war, they said. Who knows where? I've wondered where she was, and why she never came for me. Is she living or dead? I don't know." He tossed a stick onto the fire.

"If you're wondering how I escaped the slaughter—," Anabal said, "when the king ordered the death of the male babies, a Roman soldier brought me to Batitha, a childless barmaid with whom he was keeping company. She hid me until the slaughter was over."

***

Antillus cast a wary glance over his shoulder as he approached the barmaid's door. He had recited Herod's decree to Shira, and now carried a bundle wrapped in goatskin. In the bundle was a small child whom he had secretly whisked away to save him from Herod's slaughter. Antillus had sons of his own whom he longed to hold as he now held this one. The blood of this child he could not spill.

He had waited for darkness, wary that he might be discovered before he completed his mission. If so, both he and the babe would have been put to death. At Batitha's door he scanned the area for anyone who might foil his plan. Seeing no one, he rapped briefly on the door post, then rushed inside.

Batitha met him in the middle of the room.

"Here," said Antillus, placing the bundle in her arms. "You wanted a babe so bad, here's one for you."

"A babe?" she said.

"You must keep him out of sight for a time. Herod gave orders that all boy babies be killed."

"Yes, I heard." She clutched the bundle to her breast. "Why did you choose to save this one?"

"I don't know," he said with a solemn shake of his head. "Maybe it was because I had seen too many babies die already. Anyway, I didn't join the legion to murder innocent children." As he dashed away, he said, "I guess you don't need to know, but he is the son of a woman named Shira. His name is Jabal. Guard him well!"

***

"Batitha died when I was fourteen," Jabal said to Judah. "That's when she told me my mother's name was Shira."

Judah's heartbeat quickened. How far should he go in pursuit of this matter? If his judgment proved wrong, it could be harmful to both Jabal and Shira. But, if it turned out to be correct, the lives of a mother and son, who for years had been separated, might be fulfilled.

"Jabal," Judah said, "I believe my friend Shira–might have been your mother."

With a dubious shrug, Jabal said, "All I know is, she never came looking for me."

"You must remember, she thought you died in the massacre."

"You knew her?"

"Many years ago Shira and I served in the rebellion. If she was your mother, you have reason to be proud." From beneath his robe Judah brought a dagger sheathed in a silver scabbard, and held it out to Jabal.

"This once belonged to a man who was close to Shira," he said. "His name was Romulo de Vincius."

"Romulo? I've heard of him." He ran his fingertips over the intricate engraving on the sword. "Was Romulo my father?"

"No, but he would be pleased that you are safe. After Romulo died, Shira brought this sword to me. Like you, for many years I didn't know if she was dead or alive, but I've carried the dagger all this time, hoping one day to return it to its rightful owner, the woman I believe to be your mother."

"But you never found her."

"No." His eyes met those of the younger man. "Not until today. Shira bas Haran was the woman healed by the Master today beside the sea."

Jabal swallowed hard."That was my mother?"

"That was Shira bas Haran."

"Why didn't you tell me then?"

"I didn't know you then," Judah said. "Not until I heard Andrew call you by name. Now that we know she is alive, we will find her."

CHAPTER 24

In the market place at Jerusalem, Shira had told Shukar goodbye. He was off to Alexandria, and she to Bethlehem. "If my good fortune holds," he said, clasping her hands in both of his, "our paths will cross again."

"I would like that."

"Seeing you has brought joy to my life."

"God go with you, Shukie."

"And with you, Shira."

***

Hardly had Shira and Rachel settled down with their wine cups when Jason burst through the door. "They've arrested the Nazarene!" he shouted. "Caiaphas and his henchmen hauled him before Pilate. Jochai was there!"

***

Jochai, on his way to deliver a pair of sandals to Rabbi Eleazar, had grumbled to himself that the rabbi probably would not pay him this time either. But then, the thought took him back to the Baptist, who spent half his life waist deep in the waters of the Jordan River, baptizing converts "in the name of him who baptizes with the Holy Spirit!" Maybe the rabbi was right, Jochai conceded. Maybe sandal making was "something he could do" to help people of a higher calling. He threw out his chest, plastered on his face a broad smile, and continued on his way. As he rounded the corner into Eleazar's street, he was greeted by what he thought was a processional, or some kind of celebration. As he drew nearer, though, the shouting grew louder. Angry, voices told him it more likely was an unruly mob. Leading the parade were white-robed temple priests, waving their arms, shouting derisive epithets, whipping the crowd into a frenzy.

Stunned by what he saw, Jochai stopped still as a statue. A tall man in a tattered robe was being pushed and dragged by a collection of thugs. The man made no attempt to resist nor defend himself. Jochai had seen him before, but where or when? The processional surged past, and Jochai got a glimpse of the victim's face. The Nazarene! He was even closer now than when he had seen John baptize him that day in the waters of the Jordan. What had he done? Where were they taking him?

Shoved roughly aside by the pressing mob, Jochai was caught up in the raging multitude. He struggled like a leaf in a gale to regain his footing and was swallowed by the taunting mob. Along the street surged the river of human flesh. Jochai could no longer see the Nazarene, but his ears were aflame with the jeers of those who abused him.

"Hail to the king of the Jews!" some jeered.

"Crucify the blasphemer!" others shouted.

At last the wicked serpent plunged its hideous head against the iron fence enclosing the courtyard of the governor's palace.

It was the practice of Roman governors to arrive in

Jerusalem from Caesarea to maintain order during festive occasions, such as Passover celebrates earlier in the day.

Advised of the Nazarene's arrest, now near midnight, Pilate assumed his position of authority, presiding over the proceedings from an upholstered bench on the upper level of the courtyard.

A Roman guard shoved Jesus forward, causing him to stumble forward. Little stock did Pilate put in anything the Jews taught each other. Well aware of the man known as the Master, the procurator gave no more thought to the Nazarene than to others who had claimed to be the messiah. He had heard of the charges that Caiaphas and temple authorities lodged against the Nazarene, dismissing them as religious concerns of the Sanhedrin, not legal matters requiring a determination by the Roman governor. However, at the first shriek of "Crucify him!" the matter became the governor's responsibility, for the Romans had stripped the Judeans of the authority to condemn a prisoner to death on the cross.

Finally, having questioned Jesus, Pilate learned nothing that warranted crucifixion. "I find no fault in him," he said to the jeering mob.

But that did not satisfy the Nazarene's tormentors who kept shouting accusations, demanding the crucifixion of the innocent man who uttered not a word in his defense.

Pilate was reminded by an aide that it was customary in the time of Passover that a prisoner be released. "Whom shall I release to you, then," said Pilate, "the king of the Jews?"

"No!" the hostile hordes protested. "Not him! Barabbas. Give us Barabbas!"

Barabbas, convicted of murder and treason, was lauded by Judeans as a leader of opposition to Roman rule. Unleashing their derision against the Nazarene, the mob demanded that Barabbas be released.

Though convinced of the Nazarene's innocence, Pilate

was unwilling to risk being deposed by Rome if he went against the will of the people. He agreed that Barabbas be released, then called for a basin of water and plunged his hands into it, cleansing himself of responsibility in the crucifixion of the guiltless Jesus.

"His blood is on your hands!" Pilate shouted, and from the rowdy blood-seeking multitude rose a cry of victory. "Crucify!"

Guards laid hold of Jesus, beginning the cruel, humiliating process of crucifixion.

Jochai, watching the Nazarene being beaten by the soldiers, then being dragged away, grabbed the grillwork for support, sank to his knees, and wept.

Only yesterday had Jerusalem over flowed with worshipers who traveled from many lands to celebrate Passover. Even so, Jesus had grieved over what the Scriptures said was coming–that he would be put to death, and on the third day he would rise from the tomb. Last night he had joined his disciples in an upper room borrowed from a man who did not know him. Even then, after three years of teaching the truth of eternal salvation as revealed to him by his Father God, Jesus knew the end was at hand.

And now, suffering the humiliation of arrest, enduring the mockery of a pseudo trial, and the brutal punishment that the prophets had foretold, Jesus was being forced to carry the cross upon which he had been condemned to die.

CHAPTER 25

Shira hurried along the streets of Bethlehem as fast as her legs could carry her. Reaching the gate opening to the road leading to Jerusalem, she encountered crowds of pilgrims who had observed Passover at the temple in Jerusalem. Pushing her way through, someone shoved her aside and she fell to the ground. A young rabbi lifted her, helped her onto his donkey, and sent her on her way. At the Dung gate, she leaped off the donkey and ran along the street. Following the clamor of the rampaging mob, she finally reached the street where she saw the Nazarene with a crown of thorns crushed onto his brow, blood streaming down his face.

Shira's heart sank at sight of the Master laboring under the weight of the crude wooden cross. Struggling to get closer, she saw him stumble. Their eyes met briefly, hers tear stained, his sad and pleading. Then, even with the weight of the ponderous beam boring into his shoulder, Shira was sure she saw the trace of a smile touch his lips. It was as if the triumph were his, and he was at peace.

Shira reached out to him, but a guard barked at her, "Stand back!"

"Please," she cried, "let me walk with him."

"Stay where you are," came the snarled response, "or you'll join him on the cross!"

"Master!" she called.

Again her eyes met his, and through the blood flowing from his thorn embedded brow, she saw him smile. Yes, he did! Was she the only one who noticed? Was she the only one who cared? It was as though his smile were meant for her alone. As if he recognized her from when he healed her. The sadness in his eyes reminded her of Rabbi Josef who, with his last breath had said," Weep not for me, Shira, but for Judea."

Under the weight of the cross, Jesus slumped to his knees.

"You there!" a Roman guard shouted to a huge Cyrenian nearby. "Take up the cross!"

The Cyrenian lifted the cross from the shoulders of the Master who walked beside him until they reached an ugly hill called Golgotha.

A guard ordered Jesus to lie down with his back to the cross. Shira, shot through with agony for the Master, suffered the sight of Roman soldiers pounding heavy spikes into his hands and feet, ripping the flesh of him who had said, "Go in peace, good woman. Your faith has made you whole." Even as the guards lifted the cross, dropped it into a hole, and tamped the dirt around it to prevent its toppling, jeers and mockery still taunted him who came to save the world from such cruelty.

Shira's trembling lips formed the word, "Why?" Surely his persecutors could not have known him. She watched a single tear struggle down Jesus's cheek as he bade a silent farewell to the woman who someone said was his mother. Shira's heart went out to her, sharing the pain of her loss as the gentle, guiltless man nailed to the cross breathed his last, pleading, "Father, forgive them, for they know not what they do."

Shira could no longer watch the life drain from the body of the man who had made her well. With a heavy heart she trudged down the hill, her ears burning with the taunts of his tormentors.

On her way down, she felt she was being followed, sensing the eyes of someone on the back of her head. Realizing she was not alone on the path, a guarded glance over her shoulder told her that a man was matching her step for step only a few paces behind. Drawing her robe close about her, she increased her pace down the rocky path leading to the city. Now only a step or two ahead of him, she risked another frenzied glance, almost colliding with him. She opened her mouth to protest.

"Shira?" the man said. "Are you Shira bas Haran?"

"Yes," she said, trembling with fear. "I am Shira. What is it you want?"

"Please," he said, "I mean no harm."

She faced a tall man with a gray beard, his face framed in a brown mantle."I am Judah," he said. "Judah ben Hezekiah."

"Judah!" she cried, near to collapsing with relief. "You scared the life out of me!"

"I'm sorry. I only meant—"

"I heard you were alive, and I so wanted to believe it was true!"

He explained that in the battle at Herodium he had been blinded by a blow to the head.

Then what Zukar had told her was true.

"I spent many helpless years groping in darkness," he said, "even begging for alms on the streets."

"How dreadful!"

"Then one day some friends of mine helped me to the market place in Capernaum where they had heard of a man who healed the sick, made the lame to walk, and restored sight to the blind. When they told me he was near, I called out to him. He asked if I believed that he could make me see. I said, yes, Lord, I believe. He then touched my eyes with his fingertips, and when he took them away, I could see! The first thing I saw was the face of the man they nailed to that cross today!"

"Oh, Judah!" Her eyes were wet with tears; she placed a hand on his arm. "I too was healed by him. For many years I was in prison where I contracted a disease of the blood. Once free, I was encouraged by a friend–as you were–to seek the Master's help, and he took the pain away!"

Judah gave his head a thoughtful nod. "I know," he said. "I was there."

"You were there?"

"By the seashore when the Master healed you. I was so happy to see you that I wanted to run to you then, but I dared not."

She pressed a gentle palm against his face."I am so glad we found each other," she said.

"Yes. Since the Master gave me back my sight, I've been following him–and looking for you."

From his waistband he brought Romulo's dagger. "For all these years," he said, "I've carried this with me, longing for the day when I could return it to its rightful owner, without knowing whether I would see you again." He held the sword out to her.

"Romulo's sword!" she said.

"He would want you to have it."

With trembling fingers she accepted the dagger that set her mind awash in a sea of memories of the man who, with his dying breath, had gasped her name.

"And now," said Judah, "now that we have found each other–"

In his pleading eyes she saw the same longing with which she had lived for so long–the need for the nearness of someone dear to her. A hand to touch and to touch her, a compassionate voice of one with whom she could share the joy of being alive. His eyes, his speech, and his gentle manner told her that Judah ben Hezekiah yearned for the peace and comfort that only she could give.

"Judah," she said, "wherever you are is where I want to be." Taking one of his hands in both of hers, she pressed it to her cheek. "Wherever you go, Judah ben Hezekiah, I will be at your side."

"Until now," he said, his eyes bright with relief and hope, "because we both loved Romulo, I could say nothing. But, now I can tell you, since the first time I came to your home,

I have dreamed of this moment." He drew her to him, then abruptly released her.

"What, Judah? What is it?"

"There is a matter that I must tell you of. A young man–"

"Yes? A young man–"

"A follower of Jesus. His name is Jabal."

"Jabal? His name is Jabal?" She was beside herself with excitement.

"He was there by the seashore when the Master healed you. He and I had never met, but

I later heard one of the disciples call him by name. From what Jabal told me– I think it would be good if the two of you met. Shira, I believe Jabal may be your son."

"My son!" She could hardly speak.

But wasn't Jabal slain with the other innocents? Her lips quivered, her eyes filled with tears.

"My son Jabal! Where? How? Tell me, Judah!"

Gently he cupped her face in his hands.

"I will take you to him," he said.

A sudden clap of deafening thunder shook the earth, shocking bolts of lightning shattered the sky, and torrents of blood-red rain flooded the streets of Jerusalem, and there was darkness on the face of the earth.

Judah quickly wrapped Shira in his cloak.

"Come, Shira," he said. "We must find shelter."

***

Judah and Shira reached the disciples' camp on the outskirts of Jerusalem. News of Jesus's crucifixion swept the land like a blast of winter wind. Disciples and converts huddled in small groups around campfires, mourning, consoling each other in hushed voices. Some wept openly, others knelt in prayer, all were burdened with sadness for the death of their Master.

Many asked themselves, and each other, why they had not gone with Jesus to Golgotha? Simon Peter had vowed to die with him, but had not been there when the spikes were pounded into the hands and feet of the Master he worshiped? Why had they not stood up to his persecutors, letting Jesus know that they loved him, believed he was the Son of God, and that he was still their Master? Would it have been different had they done so? Only one disciple, known to Jesus as John the Beloved, witnessed the horror of the crucifixion, into whose hands Jesus had commended his mother.

Jabal was sitting alone at a small fire when he saw Judah walking toward him. With curious wonder about the woman at Judah's side, he got to his feet. "Is that you, Judah?" Jabal said.

"Yes," said Judah. "And I have brought someone with me."

Jabal stared for a long moment at the woman whom Judah had said might be his mother.

"Jabal?" Shira said, struggling to maintain composure.

"I am Jabal," he said.

"I am Shira bas Haran," she said. "I once had a beloved son named Jabal."

Judah slipped away as they talked.

"Won't you sit down?" Jabal said. He set a wooden stool for her beside the fire.

"I–I– believed you were– Herod's decree–"

"I know about that. You thought I was dead. Judah told me."

"Yes. And Judah told me about Batitha," said Shira, "I am so grateful for her."

"I knew she wasn't my mother, but when you never came for me, I thought you didn't want me."

"Please– We have so much to talk about." She put a trembling hand to her mouth, covering wracking sobs. "I lived for you, Jabal. Except for memories of you that I have relived over and over for all those years in prison, I might have died there."

They fell silent, alone with thoughts of their own.

"You were in prison?" Jabal said then.

"Yes, for many years. There will be time enough to tell you about that."

Does he believe me? she asked herself. *What if he no longer needs me? He has another life now. What if he doesn't want me after all these years?*

She is a gentle woman, Jabal counseled himself. *She so wants to believe that I am her son. Do I believe I am? It may take some time.*

"I am so glad we found each other," he said. "Would it be all right if I called you mother?"

"Oh, Jabal!" Shira cried, reaching for him. "How I have longed to hear that word." She drew him to her, and he wrapped her in his arms. "Yes!" she said, her eyes aglow. "Call me Mother!"

ABOUT THE AUTHOR

An accomplished author with many books to his credit, David A. Estes draws on his wide experience, from the cotton fields of Oklahoma and Texas where he grew up, to the islands of the South Pacific where he served as a United States Marine, to the market place in America where he retired from a career in broadcasting.

David writes westerns and mysteries, along with many other genres of novels and short stories. He lives on his family farm in West Central Missouri with two black Labs and a suspicious cat.

OTHER PUBLICATIONS BY DAVID A. ESTES

Available at amazon.com, barnsandnoble.com, abebooks.com and other online retailers.

Angel on My Back
Wet Dogs Don't Ride
Bye Bye, Sweet Susie
A Bag of Gold
Ajax and Elbow Grease

Coming Soon:
Short Story Anthology
Nicodemus